Readers love the Tucker Springs series

Where Nerves End

"*Where Nerves End* was a breathtakingly beautiful story, full of angst, passion and coming out… I loved this story."

—TTC Books and More

Second Hand

"This was an enjoyable read with a very satisfying happily ever after. I loved seeing Paul come into his own and choose El above all others."

—Open Skye Book Reviews

Dirty Laundry

"As with any Heidi Cullinan book, there are feels galore and this one will hit you in the heart more than a few times."

—Diverse Reader

Covet Thy Neighbor

"Watching these two navigate this relationship is a fantastic journey for the reader. This is such a great addition to the Tucker Springs world."

—Paranormal Romance Guild

By L.A. WITT

Rules of Engagement • Rain

TUCKER SPRINGS
Where Nerves End
Covet Thy Neighbor
After the Fall

WRENCH WARS
Last Mechanic Standing
Wrenches, Regrets, & Reality Checks

Published by DREAMSPINNER PRESS
www.dreamspinnerpress.com

AFTER THE FALL

L.A. WITT

REAMSPINNER
PRESS

Published by
DREAMSPINNER PRESS

5032 Capital Circle SW, Suite 2, PMB# 279,
Tallahassee, FL 32305-7886 USA
www.dreamspinnerpress.com

This is a work of fiction. Names, characters, places, and incidents either
are the product of author imagination or are used fictitiously, and any
resemblance to actual persons, living or dead, business establishments,
events, or locales is entirely coincidental.

After the Fall
© 2019 L.A. Witt

Cover Art
© 2019 Reese Dante
http://www.reesedante.com
Cover content is for illustrative purposes only and any person depicted
on the cover is a model.

Mass Market Paperback ISBN: 978-1-64108-130-6
Trade Paperback ISBN: 978-1-64080-910-9
Digital ISBN: 978-1-64080-909-3
Library of Congress Control Number: 2019932252
Mass Market Paperback published December 2019
v. 1.0
Trade Edition previously published by Riptide Publishing, October
2013.

Printed in the United States of America
∞
This paper meets the requirements of
ANSI/NISO Z39.48-1992 (Permanence of Paper).

CHAPTER ONE

Y<small>ESTERDAY</small>, <small>AFTER</small> ten years of dreaming, three years of saving, and almost a full year of searching for the perfect horse, I finally bought Tsarina. Today, after six and a half hours squirming behind my desk, I didn't hesitate when Mike said, "Nathan, get out of here. Enjoy your ride."

I clocked out and burned rubber getting from the Light District to the edge of the foothills and down the dusty driveway to the farm where I boarded Tsarina.

And here we were, Tsarina plodding lazily down a shady trail while I watched a few flecks of sunlight playing on her black mane and dappled black-and-bronze coat. My saddle creaked softly in time with the hoofbeats on the dirt, the sound almost hypnotic. The ranch had faded behind us, and now it was just her and me out here in the woods. *Finally.*

This was all I had planned for the summer. Classes were out, and Tsarina and I were going to spend the summer getting to know each other on the trails. Come winter, we'd start working with a trainer and set our sights on competition, because a big, smooth-moving Trakehner like Tsarina belonged out on the dressage circuit.

For the time being, though? I'd take it easy with her and enjoy the fact that I finally had a horse again.

Now that she was sufficiently warmed up from the gentle walk and a few short trots, I decided to pick up the pace. I tapped her with my foot and clicked my tongue, and Tsarina immediately flowed from a walk into a perfectly smooth, rocking-horse canter. I couldn't help grinning. From my limited experience with her, I was convinced this mare was physically incapable of a choppy gait.

Grinning even bigger, I wondered what she'd be like when she had free rein to drop the hammer and *go*. How fast, how smooth—how did she run when she wasn't fenced in?

I couldn't resist.

As the incline steepened on a straightaway, I stood in the stirrups, leaned over her neck, and urged her on with my knees. She didn't hesitate, launching into a full gallop like she'd been shot from a cannon.

Her mane whipped at my face. I squinted against the wind. God, but she was smooth. Like one of those horses you can ride while holding a glass of champagne and not spill a drop. *Perfect*.

The trail got steeper, and she ran harder to make it up the slope.

I heard the engine a split second too late.

A blue-and-white motorcycle shot out from the right.

Tsarina shied. The biker skidded sideways, like we'd startled him as much as he'd startled us. Dirt sprayed in the air. My horse tried to spin one way. Then she whipped back the other way. I'd almost recovered from my own startle enough to keep my balance, but then she jerked sideways again, and I knew that panicked, weightless sensation all too well, that moment when *oh shit* becomes *I'm falling*.

Worse.

I'm falling became *we're falling*.

Me and all sixteen-plus hands of her.

I had just enough presence of mind to pull my foot out of the stirrup before we hit the ground, but I landed hard enough to knock the wind out of me. Tsarina landed on my leg. Nothing hurt, but that wouldn't last. Not with that crunch that hadn't yet registered in my—

Oh God. There it is.

I tried to curse but still couldn't breathe.

Tsarina scrambled to her feet. I reached for the dangling reins but closed my fingers around nothing. Then an eye-watering wave of pain in my leg sent me right back to the ground.

Over the idling motorcycle engine, hoofbeats.

I forced myself up onto my elbows. My heart jumped into my throat as Tsarina ran like hell the way we'd come, leaf-filtered sunlight flickering across her glossy hide.

I tried to call her name. Still couldn't get the air moving.

Panic. My lungs. My horse. My *leg*.

Couldn't walk. Couldn't breathe. Couldn't see or hear Tsarina.

I coughed, forcing some air to move.

Footsteps hurried toward me, reminding me I wasn't alone. Pain and panic retreated to make room for fury. *Son-of-a-bitch reckless motorcyclist.*

A hand pressed down on my shoulder. "Hey, you all right?"

I didn't realize I'd moved at all until the biker stumbled backward, holding one side of his face.

"Son of a bitch!" I grabbed my wrist as pain exploded up from my knuckles.

He stared at me, rubbing his face. "What the—"

"I need to find my horse before she gets hit by a car." Again I started to get up, but again the excruciating pain in my leg stopped me. "Oh. *God.*"

"Take it easy." He put a hand back on my shoulder. "How bad is it?"

"Bad enough I'm not walking out of here." I fumbled to get my cell phone out of my pocket. "But I need to find my—*fuck.*" I withdrew my hand, grimacing and wondering why the fuck *that* hurt so bad too.

"You need to sit there and not move." The authoritative tone gave me pause. I looked up at him. Blood from his nose darkened the left side of his light brown goatee.

Oh. Right. That's *why my hand hurts.*

I tried to flex my fingers, but... no. Shit. That wasn't good.

"Listen." He kept a hand on my shoulder, dabbing at his nose and mouth with his other glove. "I'm going to call an ambulance, but there's no way they'll find you up here, so I'll have to go down to the trailhead to meet them. Will you be all right on your own?"

I swallowed. My anger quickly deflated in favor of pain and a million worst-case scenarios about Tsarina. Where was she? Was she all right? There were two busy streets between the trailhead and the barn. Was she already gone when my name hadn't even dried on her papers yet? A lump rose in my throat. A moment of recklessness, and now she could very well be—

"Hey." The biker squeezed my shoulder. "Will you be all right on your own? I'll come back as soon as I can."

I nodded but didn't say anything.

I heard him make the call. Vaguely made out phrases like "horse fell on top of him" and "I'm pretty sure he hurt his leg," but I was listening to the wind, searching for some sign that Tsarina hadn't gone far. Some hoofbeats. A quiet sneeze. Anything. *Give me something, Tsarina.*

"They're on their way," he said after a moment. "ETA was fifteen minutes or so, and the trailhead's not far." He paused. "Do you need a jacket or anything?"

"It's fucking June," I snapped. "Just *go.*"

He hesitated, and I could have killed him when he started unzipping the padded blue-and-white jacket—*matches your bike, how adorable.* He set it beside me. "In case you need it." Then he picked up his helmet off the ground. "I'll be back as soon as I can."

I nodded but avoided his eyes.

He fired up the bike again, and a moment later he was gone. I was alone.

And in spite of the heat of the afternoon, I started shaking. Fuck. I knew what was coming. I hadn't been thrown too many times in my life, but the post-fall adrenaline crash was hard to forget: that moment when the initial panic was over and the body had to do something with all that pent-up energy. I took a couple of deep breaths but didn't bother fighting it.

When the shakes hit, I desperately needed to walk off that restless trembling, but I couldn't. Not when I was 95 percent sure one of my shaking legs was broken in at least two places.

It would pass. It always did. Probably not as fast as I'd have liked, since I had to stay still instead of walking, but it *would* pass.

I closed my eyes and took some more slow, deep breaths. My heart was racing, another symptom of that crash, and I reminded myself over and over that it would slow down, that there was nothing to freak out over, though it was hard as hell not to freak out with a heart rate like that. My hands shook in my lap. I just gritted my teeth and tried to hold my injured hand and leg as still as possible.

I glanced at the biker's jacket. It wouldn't help; I was shaking, not shivering. I wasn't cold. Admittedly, I found some comfort in the fact that he'd left it behind. Though I didn't know a thing about motorcycle equipment, it was well made, leather—probably expensive. Something told me he wouldn't leave it here and run for the hills. I didn't know his name, didn't have his insurance information, and I'd punched him. He could have disappeared and left me to find my own way home.

But the blue-and-white jacket lying crumpled in the dirt with a faint smear of blood on the collar was an unspoken promise that he really would come back.

I wasn't cold, but I dragged the jacket a little closer anyway. Carefully, I tucked it against my shaking knee to stabilize my injured leg.

The woods were almost completely silent. Wind rushed through the leaves, the odd bird chirped from somewhere outside my line of sight, but the forest was otherwise quiet. The motorcycle engine had faded into nothing, and I couldn't hear any sirens.

No horses either.

I scrubbed my uninjured hand over my face, swearing softly into the stillness.

Ten years of dreaming. Three years of saving. Almost a full year of searching for the perfect horse. Six and a half hours squirming behind my desk.

And now this.

CHAPTER TWO

I HAD no idea how much time passed. Pain and fear have a weird way of warping time and space, and I could've been sitting there for an hour before the bike's engine broke the silence again.

In spite of having his jacket beside me and being fairly certain he'd be back for that at least, the fact that the biker had come back at all was a huge relief. For all I'd known, he could've had a dozen of these jackets at home. Or he could've bitten the bullet and bought a new one if it meant he didn't have to put himself back at the scene of our little incident.

But there he was. He didn't seem to be in any hurry this time, coming up the trail at a reasonable, sane speed.

Oh, now *you're going to ride slowly and carefully. Fucking douche bag.*

He also wasn't alone. Someone was on the bike behind him. As they came closer, I recognized the light blue uniform shirt and dark blue pants, not to mention the patch on his shoulder with that weird snake-wrapped-around-a-pole symbol.

Paramedic. Thank God.

He had one of those hard plastic neck braces around his arm too, and I suppressed a groan. Those things sucked. Maybe not as bad as a busted-up leg and a throbbing hand, but this parade didn't need any more rain clouds, goddammit.

The medic got off the bike and shrugged a small pack off his shoulders. Behind him, the biker turned around and headed back down the trail.

"You're in pretty good shape for someone who had a horse fall on him," the medic said, chuckling.

"Thanks," I said. "I guess being conscious is a start, right?"

"Trust me." He knelt in the dirt beside me and set the pack on the ground. "The fact that you're sitting up and not screaming in pain is a damned good sign."

"Uh, yeah, I hope so. You see this stuff a lot?"

"More often than I'd like to admit." He slid the collar off his arm. "Before I do anything else, I'm going to stabilize your neck."

"Okay." This day just kept getting better and better.

After he'd put the collar on, securing it so it dug uncomfortably into my jaw and collarbones, he had me lie back on the dirt.

"We'll have you on a backboard as soon as possible," he said. "Stay as still as you can, all right?"

I couldn't nod, so I muttered an affirmative, and he went through all the other motions. Vitals. Questions. Checking for pain or numbness in my fingers and toes. Having me track his finger with my eyes. The usual routine.

About the time he'd determined I wasn't in any immediate danger except for the slim—but better safe than sorry—possibility of a spinal injury, the biker returned with another medic riding behind him. A pair of EMTs arrived on foot a few minutes later, one with a backboard and the other with a larger medical supply kit.

All but one of the EMTs focused on me. The fourth dug a cold pack of some variety from their kit and checked the biker's face. Most of the blood was dry now, and his nose didn't seem to be bleeding anymore, but he flinched when the EMT dabbed at the corner of his mouth.

One of the medics carefully checked out my hand. Brow furrowed, she glanced at the biker, who was now pressing the ice pack to the left side of his face. Then she turned back toward me, lifting an eyebrow.

I didn't say a word.

The other two medics stood aside and discussed—I assumed—my condition in hushed tones. Meanwhile, the other EMT finished cleaning some of the blood off the biker's face. When the biker winced, I did too. I wasn't violent by nature—I'd never taken a swing at anyone in my life. And to be fair, the biker hadn't startled Tsarina deliberately. It *had* been an accident.

The other medics broke their huddle. A decision had been made, apparently, and I was carefully transferred from the hard ground onto the harder backboard. They were as gentle as possible strapping my legs down, but the slightest pressure or jostling hurt so bad my head spun. Worse, the more they immobilized me, the more the rest of my body started to hurt. My back. My hips. My neck and shoulders. The leg that Tsarina hadn't landed on. I was going to feel like a bag of ass tomorrow, there was no doubt about it.

The medics each took a handle of the backboard, two on either side of me, and after one gave a count of three, they lifted the board and set it in a basket of some kind. It reminded me of the kind I'd seen dangling from helicopters in search-and-rescue videos, and I quickly shoved *that* image out of my mind.

My stomach twisted and turned, and it only got worse when we started down the steep trail. The medics kept me horizontal and went slowly, but I was far too aware of that sharp incline. Even my horse hadn't been able to keep her footing on it once she'd lost her balance. I didn't like this. Not at all. I was bound to the point of being in more pain than before, especially thanks to that cervical collar that could go straight to hell, but confinement terrified me. Being restrained and at the mercy of someone else—no. Just no. And right now, the added fear that I could fall again wasn't helping matters. The solid board beneath me wasn't enough to negate the precarious sensation of being off the ground. All it would take was one guy's hand slipping off. With the way my day was going, I wouldn't have been surprised if that happened.

The dull thud of hooves on dirt, accompanied by the squeak of a saddle, made my stomach tighten.

That should be me.

God, where is Tsarina?

"Whoa," a familiar voice said, and the horse stopped. So did the guys carrying my backboard. "Nathan?"

I opened my eyes, but the first thing I saw wasn't a person peering down at me. The long, mostly black face with the white star between big brown eyes sent an unbelievable rush of relief through me. "Tsarina. Thank God." My arms were strapped down—*oh, God, I can't*

L.A. Witt

move—so I couldn't reach up to pet her, but just seeing her calmed me down.

Cody, the owner of the ranch where I boarded Tsarina, swung himself off the saddle. "Your girl came runnin' up the driveway without you. Figured something must've happened." He tugged her back a little and took her place beside me. "You okay, kid?"

"Uh, I've had better days."

"I see that." He absently stroked Tsarina's muzzle. "Well. We'd better let these folks get you to the hospital. I'll follow you all down."

The EMTs kept walking. I couldn't see Cody, Tsarina, or the biker, but I could hear footsteps, hooves, and the quiet sound of the motorcycle's tires rolling over the soft ground. All the way down the trail, no one spoke. Occasionally the medics would stop so one or another could adjust their grip, but otherwise it was a long, silent trek to the trailhead.

At the end of the trail, they set me down long enough to get the stretcher out of the waiting ambulance. Then they lifted me again. I'd never imagined I'd be so relieved to find myself on a stretcher, but the minute the guys set me down this time, I swore my blood pressure dropped several notches. No more precariousness. Thank fuck. I still couldn't move, but this was an improvement. Now I could focus on things like how much my goddamned leg hurt.

Cody appeared beside me and squeezed my arm. "I'm going to go back to the barn and put Tsarina away, and then I'll come give you a lift home."

"Thanks."

He gave a slight nod. To the paramedics, he said, "You taking him to Methodist or Memorial?"

"Memorial," one said. "Let me get your name, and I'll make sure they let you in to see him."

Cody gave his information to the medic. Then he hoisted himself back onto Tsarina. "See you at the ER, kid. Hang in there."

"Will do."

He and Tsarina left, and the medics moved the stretcher into the back of the ambulance. The doors slammed behind me, and I closed my eyes. I was still in pain like nobody's business, but at least my horse was okay. Right then, there wasn't much more I could ask for.

IF THERE was one thing I hated about hospitals, it was the endless waiting. Okay, it was better than the alternative; being first in line at an emergency room usually meant a shovel sticking out of your skull or something. But sitting on the hard exam table, both bored out of my mind and nervous about what the doctor would say when he finally came in, was not my favorite way to spend an afternoon.

I closed my eyes and rubbed my face with the hand that wasn't fucked-up.

I'd already been down to radiology to have everything X-rayed. There was no way my leg would be good as new after staying off it for a few days and maybe icing it a bit. This was bad. Real bad. And the way my throbbing hand was swelling up and didn't want to move? That wasn't promising either.

At least I wasn't tied down to the board anymore. The doc had decided I didn't have any spinal injuries, which was the biggest concern, so they'd let me off the board and taken off the cervical collar. The damage was done—I was sure I had more spasms happening than I had muscles—but I could move and stretch any body parts that were willing or able to move. I could deal with the stiffness and pain. Sort of.

A nurse came in for the umpteenth time to make sure I was doing okay. As she checked my vitals, she glanced at my hand and scowled but didn't say anything.

I self-consciously tucked that hand against my side. Not that I could hide it, but that didn't stop me from trying. Every time someone examined my hand, I was sure they could tell what had happened. As if there were some sort of CSI-style animation playing in their minds demonstrating how my unscathed fist had collided with the biker's face and done whatever damage now lurked underneath my skin. Or his. I wanted to explain to every one of them that I hadn't meant to hit him. That was not like me. *So* not like me!

What if he presses charges? Could I go to jail *for that?*

No wonder all the nurses kept eyeballing my blood pressure and heart monitor. Between the last few shakes of the post-fall crash and my certainty that the cops would be here any minute to haul me away for assault and battery, I was a cardiac basket case.

The nurse left. I rolled my stiffening shoulders and tilted my head from one side to the other while I waited for the doctor to come back in. This wasn't my first rodeo, as it were, so I knew what was coming. I could already hear the orders: *Ice, not heat. Don't lift anything heavier than twenty pounds. Take two of these and don't operate heavy machinery. Ice, not heat. I'm serious, Nathan. Ice.*

Yeah, yeah. Fuck you. Heat feels better. Bite me.

Out in the hall, a female voice said, "He's right in here."

"Thank you." Cody. The door opened and he stepped in, holding his dusty baseball cap in his hands. "How you feeling?"

"Like I tried to catch a twelve-hundred-pound animal with my leg," I grumbled.

He laughed. "Least your sense of humor's intact."

"Eh, more or less."

"Keep your chin up, kid. Could've been a lot worse."

I shuddered, which hurt. Of course. "Believe me, I know."

"By the way, there's, um." He paused, glancing at the door as he cleared his throat. "That kid with the motorcycle. He's out in the waiting room. He'd, uh, like to see you."

I rubbed my eyes. He wasn't all that high on my list of favorite people right now, but... oh, what the hell. "Sure. Not like I have anything else to concentrate on at the moment."

Cody left the room. A moment later he returned with the biker, and then excused himself to go find some coffee. Bastard.

The biker and I stared at each other in uncomfortable silence. Though the air between us was tense, this was the first time I'd had a chance to really look at him, and looking at him beat the hell out of dwelling on the fact that this was nauseatingly awkward.

His nose was a little swollen, as was the corner of his mouth, but the blood was gone from his immaculately trimmed goatee. His pants were the same armored style as the blue-and-white jacket he had draped over his arm. The extra padding in the thighs only emphasized his slim waist and incredibly fit torso, especially since all he was wearing above the belt was a skintight, black Under Armour shirt.

Clearing his throat, he moved the jacket in front of him and folded both arms under it. "So. Um." He gulped. "Listen, I wanted to apologize. I didn't realize that was a bridle trail. It's—" He shook his head. "I don't know the trails that well yet."

"Neither do I." I sighed. "Probably won't get to know them this summer."

He winced. "Sorry."

Guilt formed a ball of lead in my gut. "It's all right. Like you said, you... you didn't know the trails." I shrugged with one shoulder. "It happens, I guess. One of the hazards of a multiuse trail."

"Still, I'm sorry. And, uh, by the way, my name is Ryan." He extended his hand.

"I'll have to skip the handshake." I held up my tightly wrapped hand.

"Oh. Right." His cheeks colored, and he withdrew the offer.

"My name's Nathan, though." I paused. "So, are you, um, going to...." I held up the injured hand again. "Press charges?"

"Press—" He blinked. "What? No. No, of course not."

I exhaled. "*Thank* you."

He laughed. "I was a little worried you might press them against me, to be honest."

"If you'd asked me while I was still sitting in the dirt, I might've." I laughed too. "But I guess we're kind of even."

"Even?" He ran a glance over me, and damn it, my skin tingled like that glance had been an actual touch, a hand grazing me through the thin white blanket. The things anxiety did to me, apparently. Unaware that I was an inch closer to losing my mind, Ryan met my eyes. "You're going to be in a world of hurt for a while.

I'm"—he touched his lip gingerly—"just going to be telling bar brawl stories for a few days."

I laughed again. "For what it's worth, I really didn't mean to coldcock you like that. I thought my horse was gone, and you were the closest thing, and…."

"It's okay." He smiled, though the bruised corner of his mouth didn't rise as high as the other. "Really." He held my gaze, then lowered his eyes and cleared his throat. "Anyway, I wanted to stop in and make sure you were all right. See if there was anything I could do."

"Thanks. I appreciate it."

Awkward silence fell, punctuated by the steadily accelerating beep coming from my heart monitor.

You're not helping, you stupid piece of machinery.

"She's a beautiful horse, by the way," he said. "And I'm really glad she's okay."

"Me too. Just not sure what I'm going to do with her this summer now."

"What do you mean?"

"She's in perfect condition. A few months of not riding her? She'll start losing that." I scratched my neck. "I'll figure something out."

"Maybe, um…." The padded leather jacket and pants creaked softly as Ryan shifted his weight. "Well, maybe we can make a deal."

I eyed him. "What do you mean?"

"I'm the reason you're…." He gestured at my leg. "And the reason she won't be getting any exercise. Seems like I should do something to make that up to you."

It took a moment for the pieces to pull together in my head. "Are you offering to ride her for me?"

"Well." He cleared his throat again. "If you'll teach me to ride, yes."

My first instinct was a protective "absolutely *not*." Let a novice touch my beautifully fit and still somewhat green horse? Not a chance.

But I hesitated. "You ever ridden before?"

Ryan nodded. "A little. My grandparents had horses. I rode once in a while when I visited but never really learned to do anything more than stay on."

I snorted. "You're one up on me today."

Cheeks coloring again, he laughed cautiously. "Sorry."

"No, I'm sorry. That was a cheap shot."

"Not really." He smiled a little. "I think you'd have stayed on just fine if I hadn't come along."

"Guess we'll never know."

Awkward silence descended again.

I played with the coarse edge of the blanket to occupy my good hand. "Well, if you're serious, I could definitely use the help. Fair warning, though, I'm planning to compete with her eventually, so I'll be strict as hell."

The smile he gave me was the most genuine one I'd seen on him so far. "I wouldn't expect any less."

"Good. Good. Well, uh, I should get your number." I picked up my phone off the stack of clothes that hadn't been cut off. Out of habit, I went to press the button with my right thumb, but the stiff splint and tight bandages kept me from making that mistake.

Ryan held out his hand. "I can enter it, if that's easier."

Great. Couldn't do a simple thing like put a goddamned number into my phone. Gritting my teeth, I gave it to him.

He quickly put in his contact information, then texted his own phone from mine. He handed my phone back, and I set it in my lap.

"So, you're going to compete with her, you said?"

I nodded. "Hopefully. She's not trained yet, but she's got a lot of potential."

"Not trained?"

"Well, she's broke. Rock steady under saddle. Just needs to start working toward being a dressage horse."

"Oh, you're going to do dressage with her?"

"Yep."

"Sweet." He rested a hand on top of the monitor, probably trying to do something besides fidget. "I don't know the first thing about it, but I'd love to learn."

"This might be your chance, then."

"Awesome. Well, uh, in the meantime, good, uh, good luck with…." He waved a hand at my leg. "I hope it's better than it… uh…." His cheeks darkened again.

I laughed. "I know what you meant. Hopefully it's better than it feels."

"Something like that, yeah." He took a step toward the door. "I'm going to take off, but text me or call me. About riding. I'm happy to help you keep her exercised for the summer."

I managed a smile. "Thanks."

We held each other's gazes for a long, awkward moment. I thought he might say something else. I thought I might say something else. Anything I could think to say, though, would've made it even more awkward, and I didn't imagine he had anything more eloquent up his sleeve right then.

"Well." He took another decisive step. "I'll talk to you soon."

Okay, so that was better than anything I'd come up with.

"Yeah. Talk to you soon."

And then he was gone.

Alone in the room with the incessantly beeping monitor, I stared at the phone sitting in front of me on the hospital blanket.

So the guy who'd scared my horse out from under me was now a contact on my phone. And while I recovered from my injuries, I'd teach him to ride.

Wasn't today just full of surprises?

CHAPTER THREE

WHEN I got out of Cody's car at my apartment, I came to the conclusion that crutches and a broken hand were a sick cosmic joke.

Especially since I lived on the goddamned seventh floor.

Fuck.

At least I could walk. Well, sort of. Thanks to my broken hand, I could only use one crutch, but with some work, I could get around on my own. That wouldn't have been the case if I'd taken them up on the wheelchair they'd offered me. *That* had been a brief conversation.

"We could get you a wheel—"

"Hell to the no."

"Nathan, you—"

"*No.*"

So here I was, facing my apartment with a crutch under my arm, silently cursing evolution for not giving humans wings. Getting up those stairs on my own? Not a chance. Just… no. And the thought of needing someone to help me with something as simple as stairs made my skin crawl. There was nothing in the world I hated more than leaning on someone else, never mind doing it both figuratively and literally. Christ. I'd not only lost a summer with my horse, I'd lost my independence for a few months. Fuck my life.

"This will be fun," I said. "Two casts versus six flights of stairs."

"Six flights? Oh Lord." Cody shook his head, chuckling. "This is not your day, is it?"

"Not even a little," I grumbled.

"I don't suppose there's an elevator."

"Nope." Indeed there wasn't. Not in this older-than-the-hills building. Why did I live in an apartment with no mechanical means of getting up to my front door? Because Nathan-from-the-past had thought walking up and down the stairs every day with no easy escape via an elevator would be good exercise and keep him from getting out of shape when he slacked off on going to the gym.

Hey, Nathan-from-the-past? Nathan-of-the-present and Nathan-of-the-next-three-months both think you're a dick.

I suppose if I take it really slowly, I could get to the top on my own.

"Well," Cody said, "let me help you to the top for now."

I was too tired and in too much pain to be stubborn, so I didn't argue.

Even with his help, the climb was hell. Every movement jarred my leg, and three separate times, I instinctively reached for the railing when I lost my balance, and each time I smacked that cast and sent fresh pain vibrating through my hand. The broken bones weren't the only things hurting either; at least a dozen bruises had already formed on my hip, my elbow, and my upper thigh, and I was pretty sure the stirrup had bitten pretty hard into my ankle. Good thing I'd taken my foot out of it, though. Getting dragged behind Tsarina would have made this day *so* much better.

Finally Cody and I made it to the top. I leaned against the wall to catch my breath.

"You okay?" he asked.

I nodded. "Yeah. Just need a second."

"Take your time."

When I'd recovered a little, I leaned on my crutch and hobbled toward my door.

"You got your keys?" Cody asked.

Reaching into my right pocket with my left hand while leaning on a crutch probably wasn't the most dignified thing I'd ever done, but I managed to get my keys out.

Right then, though, the door opened. Naturally.

Brad, my roommate, stared at me. His dark hair was wet and unruly, so he must have just gotten out of the shower. "Dear God. What did you *do*?"

Cody chuckled and patted my arm. "I'll let you tell him the story. Let's get you in and situated."

"Thank you," I muttered.

Brad and Cody helped me into the apartment and onto the couch. I tried not to curse at either of them while they arranged my leg on top of a stack of pillows. Easier said than done, of course. Who knew a broken bone would *hurt* so goddamned much?

Then Cody handed off the care and feeding instructions from the ER to Brad. "Make sure he keeps that leg elevated whenever he's sitting, and make him move around once in a while."

Brad saluted with two fingers and set the ER instructions on the coffee table.

Cody gently clapped my shoulder. "Take it easy, kid."

"Thanks. And thanks for the lift home and everything."

"Anytime. You need a thing, you give me a call, you hear?"

I nodded.

Brad showed Cody out. Then he came back into the living room, and I cringed at the thought of how pathetic I was.

"You need anything?" he asked. "Drugs? Ice? Two-by-four to the head?"

I laughed. "That last one sounds pretty appealing."

"I'm sure."

"I'm good, though. Thanks."

"No problem." He grabbed a beer from the kitchen and then sat on the recliner beside the couch, eyeing my leg. "So what in the world happened?" Before I could answer, he smirked. "Don't tell me you already got bucked off."

I held his gaze.

The smirk turned to a grimace. "Oh. Shit. *Seriously?*"

"Okay, so I didn't quite get bucked off." I tugged at the pillow under my leg, trying to get comfortable, though that was probably impossible. "Tsarina spooked on a steep slope, and she fell."

"With you on her?"

"Technically under her when all was said and done."

Brad's eyes got huge. "My God. How bad is it?"

"Bad enough to fuck up my summer," I muttered. "Fractured both bones in my lower leg." I held up my hand. "And two more fractures here."

Brad snorted. "I'd hate to see the other guy."

Uh, well.... Clearing my throat, I looked away.

"Wait." Brad hesitated. "You… you didn't actually hit someone, did you?"

"I. Um."

"Dude. What'd you do? Get in a bar fight on your way to the ER?"

"Not quite." I laughed dryly. "When Tsarina ran off, I kind of lost it, and Ryan happened to get within reach right at that moment."

Brad arched an eyebrow. "Ryan?"

"Yeah, he… he's the one who scared Tsarina. Pulled out on the trail on his motorcycle."

"And now you're on a first-name basis with this guy?"

I glared at him. "*Anyway.* Doc says I got really lucky. The dirt I landed on was soft enough to cushion the fall a little. He said if I'd landed on pavement or even some harder clay, I'd probably have to have surgery."

"Yeah, that's pretty lucky." His brow furrowed. "But let's back up a sec. Ryan?"

I groaned and rolled my eyes.

Brad pinched the bridge of his nose for a moment, then lowered his hand. "So let me get this straight. Dude scared off your horse and put you in a cast—*two* casts—and you're—"

"To be fair, the second cast was my own fault."

"Yeah, but it was *his* face that stopped your hand, so for the sake of argument, he's got some culpability there." He cocked his head. "All that, and now you're on a first-name basis with him?"

"Yes. And I'm actually going to give him riding lessons too."

Brad's mouth fell open. "Are you kidding?"

I shrugged. "Well, it'll keep Tsarina from atrophying in a pasture for three months."

"You're giving riding lessons. To a guy you just met. To a guy you clocked in the face after he broke your leg." Brad chuckled. "I can't decide if this is going to be amusing as hell to watch, or if it's going to end in disaster."

"Or both, right?"

"You said it, not me."

"Mm-hmm. Enough about him, though." I shifted as much as the casts, pillows, and pain would allow. I wasn't quite sure why I bothered trying to get comfortable, but whatever. Once I was situated again, I said, "You have any luck with Jeff today?"

Brad wrinkled his nose.

"That bad, huh?"

"It's… I mean, we both knew it was going to be a really slow, aggravating process." He sighed. "And thanks again for letting me crash here."

"Hey, anything to keep you two from killing each other. To be honest, it's probably a good thing right now. I'm going to need all the help I can get for a while." Just saying it made me cringe inwardly. God, I hated depending on people. *Hated* it. That was why I'd refused a roommate for ages, even in the days when money was tight.

I cleared my throat. "So, what happened tonight?"

He shrugged. "It wasn't bad, I guess. All things considered."

"Okay, so I'm assuming that means you weren't screaming at each other this time?"

He sat back in the recliner. "We *were* in public."

"Fair enough. But was it one of those things that would have escalated into screaming at each other if you'd been in private?"

Brad shook his head, watching his fingers playing with the seam on the arm of the recliner. "No, not this time."

"Well, that's an improvement. Isn't it?"

"I guess. And we're, I don't know." He flattened his hand on the armrest and faced me again. "I guess we're getting there."

"Meaning?"

"Meaning, we're starting to get to some of the reasons we split up in the first place. One thing at a time."

"And Jeff still doesn't want to get a counselor involved?"

Brad laughed bitterly.

"I'll take that as a no." I scratched an itch under the cast on my arm. "So what are some of those reasons you guys figured out?"

"I'll bore you with them another night. You've probably suffered enough for one day."

I chuckled. "Yeah, but at least this way it's your misery. Takes my mind off my own."

"You're a real pal, you know that?" But he took a deep breath and settled against the back of the recliner like he was trying to both relax and brace himself before he dived into the subject. "I think he's spending too much time at work. He thinks I'm trying to monopolize his time. I think buying a house together is too risky while the market's all fucked-up. He thinks I'm making excuses to put off any kind of commitment. Which then of course leads us to arguing over—"

"Wait." I put up a hand. "You guys are still arguing over commitment when you can barely stand to be in the same room?"

"Well, it is a bone of contention."

"Okay, fair enough, but I'd start with damage control at this point, you know?"

"That *is* damage control." He leaned forward and rubbed his forehead. "Ugh. I could have sworn there was a time when shit wasn't so damned complicated with him."

I picked at the edge of the cast on my hand. "This from the man who can't understand why I've sworn off getting involved with any part of a man above his belt."

"With the fuckwits you've gone out with?" He snorted. "I'd swear off men altogether."

"Exactly."

"That said"—he inclined his head—"you know not all men are like that."

"Nope, not all." I shifted a bit to accommodate my stupid casts, wondering if *comfortable* would ever happen to me again in this lifetime. "But with the way my luck has gone, I'm not interested in seeing if the third time is the charm."

"Yeah, I guess I can't blame you." He sipped his beer. As he absently ran his finger along the edge of the label, he said, "Mind if I ask something? About your exes?"

I shrugged. "Go for it."

"Why did you stay with them for so long?"

Exhaling hard, I watched my fingers playing at the cast on my arm. "If I'd known Steve was cheating on me, I'd have dumped him sooner. Gotta give the man credit, though." I laughed humorlessly. "He did know how to cover his tracks."

Brad's expression didn't change. "What about Brent, though? I mean, Jeff and I were wondering for months when you'd finally kick his ass to the curb."

I shifted my gaze away, suddenly unable to meet my roommate's eyes. I took pride in not letting anyone push me around, especially not boyfriends, and it still grated on me to think I let that dickwad berate and belittle me for the better part of a year. Especially since I now knew people had noticed. Worse, I'd defended him to a few people along the way.

"Oh, he's having an off day."

"He really is a sweetheart."

"That's just his sense of humor."

Ugh.

"I have no idea," I finally said. "But it's over now. With him and with Steve." I sighed. "And after their shit, I need a break."

"A break for how long?"

"Probably until I'm forty."

Brad laughed. "You know that's basically inviting the universe to drop Mr. Right into your life, don't you?"

"Please." I waved my good hand. "If he's really Mr. Right, then he'll show up when the timing is right too."

Brad threw his head back and laughed harder. "Oh, Nathan, Nathan, Nathan. My darling, naïve little Nathan." He eyed me, smirking again. "Let me guess: if he comes along at the wrong time, he can't possibly be Mr. Right?"

"Something like that."

"Uh-huh."

"Whatever, man."

"Mark my words, my friend. You don't want him, which is exactly why he's going to show up."

"Mm-hmm."

He eyed me like he was thinking of pushing the issue—*go ahead, Brad, tell me the same thing happened with you and Jeff*—but then glanced at the beer in his hand. "I'm going to go get another one. You want—" His eyes darted toward the white-capped orange prescription bottle on the coffee table. "Oh. No beer for you, I guess. Uh, do you want anything?"

I scowled playfully. "Well, *now* I want a beer."

"Sorry." He grimaced. "Anything else? A soda? Something to eat?"

My stomach grumbled, and it dawned on me that I hadn't eaten a thing since lunch, which had been light since I'd been excited to the point of queasy about my upcoming ride. "I don't suppose I could talk you into throwing a sandwich together, could I?" I gestured at the pill bottle. "I need to eat something with that anyway."

"Sure, absolutely." He stood and picked up his empty beer bottle. "Anything in particular?"

"There's turkey in there, I think. Nothing fancy."

"On it. Just, um, wait there."

"Damn. And here I was thinking about taking a jog around the block."

"Be my guest." He shrugged. "Can't be held responsible if your sandwich is gone when you get back."

"Hmm, well, in that case I'll wait here."

"Good idea."

He disappeared into the kitchen. I listened to him going through the motions of preparing some food, and in the otherwise silent living room, I sighed. It was good to have him here right now. I couldn't deny that.

Pity he was here for the reasons he was. It hurt like hell to watch him dealing with his crumbling relationship, and I hoped they either got it together or moved on separately before it killed them both. The two of them had been a good match. *Such* a good match. It was a damned shame the way things had fallen apart the past year or so. Neither of them was willing to let it end without a fight, but I wondered how long it would take before they finally agreed it was over. There had to come a point where even a relationship like theirs wasn't worth saving.

"I'm not ready to let it go yet," Brad had told me the night he'd moved out of their place and into mine. "There's got to be a way to make it work again. I mean, we had something really, really good."

Yeah, you did. And look at the two of you now.

My only two serious relationships had been volatile and miserable, and both had ended the way volatile, miserable relationships usually did. No police involvement or violence, fortunately—well, besides that ceramic mug I'd thrown at a wall during one of the last fights with Steve, and a picture that had fallen off the wall thanks to Brent slamming a door—but there was nothing amicable about either of those splits.

If what Brad was going through was how a happy, stable relationship eventually ended....

Fuck that. I was fine on my own.

CHAPTER FOUR

I SLEPT on the couch that night. It wasn't the most comfortable place in the apartment, but sleeping there meant I didn't have to move my busted ass from the living room to my bedroom. And with the prescription painkillers, I could have slept anywhere without complaint. Yay, drugs.

Eventually something nudged me out of a weird dream—one of those trippy-ass ones that I forgot as soon as it ended—and I blinked a few times until my eyes focused.

My phone buzzed unobtrusively on the coffee table. Swearing and grumbling in my slurred, half-awake voice, I clumsily searched for the phone with my left hand. When I'd finally convinced my eyes to focus on the screen, I groaned at the sight of two missed calls.

Then I checked the time.

9:18 a.m.

My heart stopped. I was supposed to be at work at eight.

"Shit," I muttered and quickly speed-dialed my boss.

"Tucker Springs Acupuncture," Mike said.

"Mike, it's Nathan."

"Oh, hey!" Something banged on the other end, and I guessed he'd sat up suddenly in my desk chair and smacked the armrest on the desk like I always did. "Where are you? Everything all right? You're usually here before I am." He didn't sound annoyed in the least, just concerned.

"Uh, well…." My brain was still hazy from both sleep and the painkiller that had put me to sleep, and the explanation wasn't coming easily.

"Nathan?"

I cleared my throat. "It's kind of a long story, but my ride yesterday didn't, uh, turn out quite the way I'd hoped."

"Oh shit. What happened? Are you okay?"

"I am, but…." I gnawed my lip, not sure why I was so nervous about asking when I knew damn well Mike wouldn't object at all. "I'm gonna need a few days off."

"Sure, yeah. Of course. Anything you need. How bad is it?"

"I'm pretty banged up, but it's nothing that won't heal."

"That's good to hear. Listen, the details can wait. Most important thing now is for you to get some rest and take care of yourself. I'll manage things on this end."

I closed my eyes and sighed, trying not to worry about the mountains of paperwork that would be waiting for me when I came back. "Thanks, Mike. I appreciate it."

"Anytime. And if you need any treatments, let me know."

Acupuncture wouldn't fuse the bones back together, but damn if twenty minutes of letting some needles soothe these tender muscles and calm my claustrophobic, control-freak nerves didn't sound incredibly tempting. "I'll keep it in mind. Thanks."

I didn't do much after that. My routine for the next twenty-four hours or so consisted of eating enough to take a pain pill, sleeping until that wore off, and then eating again so I could take another dose and fall asleep again. By the end of the second day, the pain was bearable enough to go a little longer between pills, and I spent more time awake and coherent.

At some point Brad let me know he'd notified a few of the neighbors so that in the event of an emergency, someone could help me. Awesome. Because being encased in plaster and stuck in my apartment wasn't fun enough without the added worry about a fire or something.

Four days after the accident, the pain was tolerable and the only thing worse than the relentless itching under the cast was the cabin fever. And the need to see Tsarina. Cody had assured me via multiple texts that she was doing fine and hadn't shown any sign of injury from the other day. Still, I wanted to see her. I hadn't waited all these years to have a horse only to stay away from her.

By the fifth day, I was recovered enough and ready to get the fuck out of this apartment before the walls closed in around me, and it all came down to the white pain pill in my palm. Take it now, and I'd spend the afternoon in a pain-free fog. Or at least, in pain but not giving a shit about it. Don't take it, and I'd spend the day hurting but with a clear head. Or rather, hurting enough to be uncomfortable, but with a clear enough head to get out of this suffocating apartment for a little while.

I glanced back and forth between the pill in my hand and the phone in the other. After some hemming and hawing, I pulled up Ryan's number on my contact list, which gave me another pause. I still wasn't sure how I felt about the arrangement we'd made to have him riding Tsarina. Then again, I wouldn't be riding anytime soon and didn't have a lot of alternatives, so I made the call.

"Hey, Nathan," he answered. "How are you feeling?"

"Better. Thanks."

"Good to hear."

An awkward silence tried to set in—how the hell do you talk to the person who put you in a cast?—so I cleared my throat. "Listen, I was wondering, are you still game for learning to ride?"

"Yeah, absolutely."

"Busy this afternoon?"

"I'm off work at three thirty. You sure you're up for it? It's only been a few days."

"I'm doing okay, actually. The worst is over, so the pain's not as bad as you might think."

"That's good to hear. Glad it's bearable." He paused. "If you're really up for it, I can come by after work and drive you to the barn."

That gave me pause. It hadn't occurred to me I still had to *get* to the barn. "You don't mind?"

"Not at all."

"Okay." I gave him the address. "See you around four?"

"I'll be there."

RIGHT ON time, a knock at the door.

"Come on in," I said.

The door opened and—

Holy hot dude, Batman.

I hadn't been in any state of mind to really check him out the other day, but I made up for lost time now. He'd traded his motorcycle regalia for a pair of relaxed-fit jeans and a faded Metallica T-shirt with the very edge of a tattoo sticking out from beneath his sleeve. His hair was damp and perfectly arranged, so he must've showered before he'd come over here—*don't imagine it, Nathan, don't imagine a single second of it.*

His boots weren't what I'd call riding boots, but they had a sharp heel, which was the important thing— if there was a mishap, his foot wouldn't go all the way through the stirrup. As much as I would have been happy to see him dragged behind my horse while I was still royally pissed off and in a world of pain, I'd calmed down considerably since then and really didn't want him getting hurt now.

Besides, he still had one hell of a bruise on the side of his face. I decided we were even.

"So how is your—" I made a circular gesture at the same region on my own face.

He gingerly touched the corner of his mouth, then shrugged. "It looks worse than it is." With a wink, he added, "That was a pretty impressive right hook."

I laughed. "Well, remind me not to do it again." I held up the cast. "This pain in the ass wasn't worth the trade-off."

"I don't doubt it. So...." He spun his keys around his finger. "Ready to go?"

"Yeah."

He didn't move. "Are you *sure* you're up to this? It doesn't have to be today."

"Trust me." I leaned heavily on my crutch. "I need to. I'm getting cabin fever like you wouldn't believe, and I need to see my horse."

"Fair enough."

I locked my apartment door behind us, hobbled two steps down the hall, stopped, and peered down the stairs. "Shit," I groaned.

"What?"

"I think going down might be a little more complicated than coming up."

"Can you make it?" Ryan eyed the stairs, then me. "Especially with only one crutch?"

"Yeah. I'll be fine. I think up until now I'd kind of blocked out the fact that there are stairs between here and the ground."

He grimaced. "Do you need some help?"

"No," I said quickly. "I've got it. I'll just… I have to figure it out. I'm going to have to get up and down these stairs in a cast for the next few months. Might as well learn sooner than later."

"Nathan." He eyed me. "You can start pushing yourself after you've healed a little. Come on. Let me help."

I gritted my teeth. "Fine."

Ryan took my crutch in one hand and put the other arm around my waist. I put my right arm around his shoulders, careful not to smack him in the face with my cast, and held the railing with my other hand.

Together, we took that first awkward step down. I distracted myself from my own helplessness by remembering who I was leaning on. Sort of like how a buddy of mine had said his appendix operation wasn't as bad as it could have been because he had a hot nurse, this was a lot easier to stomach knowing I had my arm around this particular set of shoulders. He felt like someone who spent a fair amount of time at the gym—he was naturally broad shouldered, but I had no doubt these muscles got some use.

"Jesus Christ," Ryan muttered as we neared the bottom. "I could've sworn there weren't so many steps on the way up."

I snorted. "Tell me about it."

On the ground floor, he handed the crutch back and carefully released me, not letting go until I was completely balanced. "You okay?"

"Yep." I adjusted the crutch under my arm. "I hope it won't be too much of an imposition to ask you to help me back up later tonight." God. Just asking made me cringe.

"Not at all." He held open the front door and stood aside. Once I was outside, he pulled out his keys and gestured across the parking lot. "Stay here. I'll bring the truck over."

"Thanks."

He returned a moment later in a small, beat-up pickup truck, and while the engine idled, he came around to help me get in on the passenger side.

As we pulled out of the parking lot, I spent a moment taking in all the familiar scenery. After being cooped up in my apartment for five days, it was like seeing everything—the gross drive-in across the street, the rows of office buildings along one side, and the condos slowly encroaching on the affordable apartments—for the first time. From the mountains in the distance to the dilapidated Honda that would probably always be broken down by the dumpster, all of it was a welcome, refreshing sight.

Ryan merged onto the interstate, and we headed for the foothills.

"So you said you've ridden before, right?" I asked.

He nodded. "Just, you know, goofing around."

"What is it you want to learn?"

"I don't know, to be honest. Maybe learn some of the finer points. Mostly I want to get back in the saddle and remember what it's like to ride."

"I know what you mean. Fair warning, Tsarina's still a little green herself. She's broke, and she's incredibly willing, but she's still young, and she doesn't know a whole lot yet. If you think I'm going too slow with you, keep in mind I'm going slow for her benefit too."

Ryan nodded. "Duly noted. How old is she, anyway?"

"Not quite five. I mean, it's not like she hasn't had any training, and she's pretty solid under saddle, but…."

"But she's young," he said. "I follow, don't worry." He glanced at me. "So how long have you been riding?"

"Since kindergarten. A girl in my class had a pony at her birthday party, and all it took was one little walk around the yard on him, and I was hooked."

"Ever had one of your own?"

I nodded. "I did 4-H when I was a kid. A friend leased us this Appaloosa gelding. God, he was the most cantankerous little shit I've ever ridden, but he was still fun."

Ryan chuckled. "My grandma had a horse like that. I swore that thing wanted to bite my head off every time I got near him, but he sure was a blast out on the trails."

I laughed. "Best kind of horse. I mean, I like to compete, but you'll never keep me off the trails."

Ryan responded with a not-completely-comfortable laugh. "Not permanently, anyway."

"Right." I glanced down at my cast. "Something like that."

He cleared his throat. "Well, hopefully it's only for a few months."

"Hopefully."

We exchanged glances.

Ryan kept driving.

CHAPTER FIVE

IT WAS probably the fact that the novelty hadn't worn off yet, but so far every time I'd seen Tsarina, I'd gotten that giddy, kid-on-Christmas feeling in my gut. Though I wouldn't be riding her anytime soon, I still had that feeling as Ryan and I watched Cody bring her in from the paddock.

She was gorgeous. Her previous owner had been horrible with a camera, and the photos had presented Tsarina as a disproportionate nag with zero personality. It was only her breeding that had convinced me to check her out, and my jaw had literally dropped when I saw her. She was nearly seventeen hands, and she was still young enough—about four and a half—that she might yet grow a little more. Her seal brown coat—mostly black and dark brown with some lighter brown areas—was gleaming and dappled, and she was in tip-top shape. She'd be spectacular in the dressage ring, and maybe someday if I had the money and the space, I could have her bred.

She eyed me as I hobbled toward her. Her ears pricked forward, and she lowered her head to snuffle at my cast. When she tugged at my crutch with her lip, I laughed and nudged her away. "You're going to scare yourself, baby."

Cody laughed. "This one's good at that." He glanced at Ryan. "You gonna say hello?"

I half expected Ryan to hang back or approach slowly and uncertainly. For as nervous as he could be around people, though—or at least around me—he wasn't the least bit timid as he walked up to Tsarina. He held out his hand, palm up, and approached slowly, but he didn't withdraw his hand when she stretched out her neck to sniff it. As she searched it with her upper lip, he reached up with his other hand and stroked her neck.

"You don't remember me, do you?" he said softly as he petted her. "That's probably a good thing. We didn't really get off on the right foot."

If she did remember him, she obviously didn't care that he'd been the one to scare her half to death. As far as she was concerned, people were sources of attention and treats, and Ryan was no exception.

When she nibbled at his pocket, he gently pushed her nose away. "There's nothing in there for you. Sorry."

"Not yet," I said. "If you're anything like me, you'll be keeping treats in there before long."

"We'll see." He tousled her short forelock, and she rubbed her head against his hand. "But yeah, probably."

Still holding the lead, Cody turned to me. "Want me to put her on the crossties here?" He gestured at the ropes hanging on either side of the aisle.

I nodded. "Please."

He clipped one tie to each side of her halter, and she stood patiently in the middle of the aisle. "You boys good on your own? I need to bring in turnouts before feeding."

"Yeah, we're fine," I said.

Cody left, and Ryan stood back, checking out Tsarina like he'd never seen her before. Which in a way I supposed he hadn't. The other day, there hadn't been a lot of time for admiring anything.

Horses or *men*, I thought, giving him an appreciative down-up that I hoped to God he didn't notice. Every time I looked at him, I saw less of the guy who'd scared my horse and more of the guy who would've made me do a double take if I'd seen him on the street. And nothing made a man sexier in my eyes than having a way with animals. A man who treated an animal like she had a personality, like she was something more than farm equipment with a pulse, was enough to reduce me to a quivering mess.

For that matter, Tsarina seemed to like him, which was a plus.

Why did I care? Besides, she liked everyone. And why was I checking out his ass again?

Apparently oblivious, Ryan said, "She really is gorgeous. What breed?"

"Trakehner." I rested my weight on my crutch and reached up to pet her neck. "Honestly, it's a miracle I was able to afford her."

"Is that right?"

I nodded. "They're usually expensive as fuck, but the owner hit some hard times because of the economy. He had to sell off a bunch of his stock for next to nothing. I practically stole her."

He chuckled, running the backs of his fingers down her nose. "Lucky."

"Yeah. Especially with her breeding." I grinned. "She's descended from this incredible stallion who just killed it in dressage in Germany." I nodded toward Tsarina. "Both of her parents trace back to him."

"Both of them?" He quirked an eyebrow. "Isn't that... bad for them?"

"Not when they're related that far back. And that's where her registered name comes from. Tsarevna is 'daughter of the tsar,' but 'Tsarina' isn't quite such a mouthful."

"Tsarevna," he murmured. "Cool name."

"It fits her." I patted her neck. "She sure *thinks* she's a princess."

Ryan laughed. "Can you blame her?"

"Not really. And I fully intend to spoil her rotten, so...."

"Good. Every horse deserves to be spoiled."

"They do." I gestured at the plastic tote full of grooming supplies by the wall. "Now get to spoiling her."

Chuckling again, he saluted. "Yes, sir."

I sat on one of the tack trunks pushed up against a stall door. There was no place to put my leg up for now, but we wouldn't be out here long, so I didn't worry about it.

Ryan picked up a currycomb—one of the rough rubber brushes—and started making circular motions on her coat, going against the grain to stir up the dirt and any loose hairs. When he hit a spot at her withers just below the point where her mane started, she leaned into the brush.

"That an itchy spot?" He grinned and kept scratching her with the brush. She stretched out her neck, turned her head, and twisted her lip until she resembled a camel having a stroke. When she rolled her eyes back, Ryan and I both laughed.

After a moment he stopped. Tsarina shook herself, raising a cloud of dust, and snorted.

I coughed, waving a hand to chase away the dust. "You're so dignified, darling."

"Isn't she, though?" Ryan kept currying the rest of her coat. "At least I don't do like my grandpa used to do. He thought it was hilarious to put gloves over their ears."

"Gloves? Over…?"

"Makes them look like a reindeer." He held his free hand up above his head. "Or a moose. One of the two."

I laughed again. "Oh God. I've never done that."

"It's funny as hell, especially if they keep flicking their ears back and forth." He turned to Tsarina and scratched under her jaw. "We won't do that to you, though."

"Not without a camera nearby, we won't," I said.

Ryan put the currycomb back in the tote and pulled out a soft brush. He ran that over her coat, but then something on her front leg seemed to catch his eye. He knelt beside her, running his hand down her leg.

"Something wrong?" I asked.

"She's got a little cut here," he said over his shoulder. "Is this from the other day?"

I leaned forward until I could see the scratch, which was mostly healed. "No, I think she did that the day I brought her home. She still needs some work getting in and out of the trailer."

"Oh." He stood again and checked her over slowly. "And she was… okay? After what happened on the trails?"

"Yeah." I sat back against the stall door again. "My leg cushioned her fall."

Ryan faced me, eyes wide, and I suddenly regretted the joke.

"Honestly, she was fine," I said. "Horses aren't that fragile."

"Yeah, I know, but...." He turned toward her again. Slowly, he ran his hand along her back, watching intently as his fingers glided across her shining brown coat, like he was inspecting her for bumps and bruises. "God, when I saw you both go down...."

"Ryan." When he turned, I said, "Relax. She's fine, and I'll be back on my feet in a few months."

He dropped his gaze.

"It was an accident," I said. "You know that. I know that. It sucked in the moment, but we're all okay."

"I know. I just feel so bad about what happened."

"It's done." I shrugged. "I know it wasn't deliberate." With a cautious smirk, I added, "Unlike that mark I left on your face."

He managed a quiet laugh, absently touching the fading bruise beside his mouth. "Well, I'd still hate to see you or her get hurt."

"We're both fine."

He held my gaze for a moment, and I gave him a reassuring smile. Without a word, he continued brushing Tsarina.

After he'd finished grooming her, I said, "My saddle's in the tack room." I gestured at the door on the other side of the aisle. "Rack number fourteen. Black dressage saddle. Bridle's hanging on the third hook from the door."

He disappeared into the tack room. Buckles rattled and leather squeaked, and a moment later he came out with my saddle over his arm and my bridle on his shoulder. I cringed at the scuffs and dirt still visible on the saddle's black leather but reminded myself that a vigorous cleaning would render most of it invisible. Once I had use of both hands again, it would be almost as good as new.

I took the bridle from him and held it while he gently set the saddle and pad on Tsarina's back. I was going to put on the bridle, but then I remembered the cast on my other hand and muttered a few curses. "Damn it. Putting on a bridle is a two-handed operation."

"And I have two hands." He held one of them out and smiled. "I got this."

I hesitated. "How long has it been since you've put one on?"

"A while, but it's not exactly rocket science." With a smirk, he added, "The bit goes between her ears, right?"

"Cute." It wasn't like I had much choice, though, so I handed over the bridle and stayed out of the way. The paranoid control freak in me had visions of the bit clanging painfully against Tsarina's teeth, or a buckle going in her eye, or the cavesson being cranked way too tight under her jaw. I gritted my teeth, biting back every instinctive "no, that's not how you do it" that bubbled to the surface before he'd done a thing.

Ryan unclipped one of the crossties, then unbuckled her halter, slipped it off her face, and buckled it again around her neck. Exactly the way I would have done it, so she was still tied, but her face was bare so the bridle would fit properly. For a moment he paused, eyeing the bridle as if he couldn't quite remember what to do with it. Before I could step in or say anything, though, he rested his wrist between her ears, and he kept it there as she obediently lowered her head. With his other hand, he guided the bit to her mouth, and when she didn't immediately open for it, he pressed his thumb into the corner of her lip, which was also exactly what I would have done. She relented, and the bit didn't bump her teeth at all as she accepted it and he put the bridle over her head.

She chomped happily on the bit while he adjusted the buckles.

"See?" He glanced over his shoulder at me. "Just like riding a bike."

"Don't get too cocky. You still have to get on and stay on."

"Challenge accepted." He undid the halter around her neck, letting it and the crosstie fall against the wall, and turned to me again. "Ready when you are."

I picked up my crutch.

"You need a hand?"

"Nope." I groaned and pushed myself up. "If I can't at least get up and down on my own, I'm fucked."

"Just don't hurt yourself."

"No promises." I tucked the crutch under my arm. "Arena entrance is up there on the left." I nodded down the aisle. "There's a mounting block in the middle if you need it."

"A mounting block?" He rolled his eyes. "Pfft. I can get on from the ground, thank you."

"Just making sure."

I followed them down the aisle. As he led her into the arena, I hobbled to the small set of dusty bleachers in the corner. With a little effort and cursing, I got my cast onto the bench beside me, and I leaned against the wall on one end. Wasn't the most comfortable seat in the house, but it would do.

Ryan brought Tsarina to a halt a few feet away from the bleachers. He tightened the girth and then asked over his shoulder, "Nathan, how tall are you?"

"About five seven."

He nodded and adjusted the stirrup leathers like a pro, letting each one out a notch to make up for our height difference.

He turned around and smirked at me. "So, Master. What's my first lesson?"

I laughed. "Get on. Let's see how much you already know and how many bad habits I need to break."

"Sounds like a plan." Ryan gathered the reins in one hand, rested that hand on her neck. Foot in the stirrup, other hand on the saddle, and he hoisted himself up onto her back. Holy fuck, wasn't *that* an amazing view of a gorgeous ass?

Concentrate, Nathan. Lessons, not ogling.

I concentrated, watching him get on. He even had the decency to let himself down gently, easing his weight into the seat rather than dropping unceremoniously onto my baby's spine. He adjusted the stirrups once more, letting them out another notch. Finally, he was situated. With the reins in one hand, he held them out to the right, which pressed the rein against the left side of her neck but also pulled on the left side of her bit. Naturally, she went left.

"Wait...." He scowled. "No, other way."

I laughed. "You learned to ride Western, didn't you?"

"How'd you guess?"

I gestured at his reins. "You're trying to neck-rein."

"Oh. So...." He turned to me again, eyebrows up.

I held my hands out in front of me as if I were the one holding the reins. "Hold them like this. One in each hand."

"So I don't need the cast to—"

"Shut up."

He laughed.

I rolled my eyes. "Very funny. Anyway, you want her to go left, put some gentle tightness into the left rein and twist your body to the left and *look* in that direction. Go right, the opposite."

His brow furrowed, but after a moment, he shrugged and muttered, "All right." He gathered his reins like I'd shown him, and then tugged the left rein just enough to pull on the bit. She turned her head but didn't move.

"Turn your body," I said. "Look where you want to go. And give her a little tap with your lower legs—just a *tap*!—to get her moving."

He did as he was told, and Tsarina obediently made a tight little circle to her left. When he switched, tugging the right rein and turning his torso to the right, she circled right.

"Good," I said. "Now walk around for a while. Get used to how she moves."

Ryan nodded and steered her to the well-beaten path along the arena wall.

I watched, pretending my mouth wasn't watering. He didn't have the natural, effortless posture of a competitive rider or the relaxed swagger of a cowboy, but for someone without a lot of experience, he was balanced and confident. Every now and then I had to remind him how to hold the reins—he was used to one-handed Western rather than two-handed English—but overall, he sure knew what he was doing in the saddle. Especially in a dressage saddle that was fucking *designed* for optimum posture.

It was quickly becoming apparent that Ryan was one of those guys who effortlessly made the simplest actions into something sexy. When he rode, when he drove, when he was just walking or standing, he had a relaxed air about him. He was probably damn hot on that bike of his too. Of course, what guy *didn't* look good on a bike? Still, he had sexy down to an art form. Laid-back without being apathetic, every gesture and posture underscoring an ability to go with the flow, no matter what. The bad boy minus the attitude. The kind of guy who could probably smoke and make me forget what a disgusting habit it was just because he looked so damned hot doing it.

Halfway across the arena, he turned Tsarina, and they made a small, perfect figure eight. She was a little impatient, walking fast and trying to sneak into a trot now and then, but she was young, full of energy, and she hadn't been ridden in a while, so that was to be expected. He handled her beautifully, though, quietly reminding her to walk and turning her in tight circles whenever she needed to remember who was in charge.

While I'd agreed to this and knew he'd be riding the horse I was dying to ride myself, I'd expected to be jealous and frustrated. What I hadn't expected was this ache in my chest. Well, maybe I did. Watching the two of them making their way around the arena drove the point home that I wouldn't be riding for a while. It was like watching my summer and my horse passing me by while I could do nothing but sit back and let it go.

There'd be time, though. There'd be next spring and next summer. We'd have the fall and the winter to work here in the arena, insulated from the bitter wind and snow. This was temporary.

Temporary or not, it still sucked, and though I'd reassured Ryan that what had happened was purely an accident, I had to admit part of me still wanted to be angry with him for putting me in this situation. He'd been going too fast. Ridden off a marked motorcycle

trail and onto a bridle trail. Damn near got Tsarina and
me both killed.

But it *hadn't* been deliberate. The punch I'd thrown
hadn't been deliberate either—or at least not premed-
itated in any kind of rational way—and he seemed to
have forgiven me for that. It was nothing more than a
case of incredibly bad timing, both of us being in the
wrong place at the wrong time, and he'd obviously
meant no harm to me or to my horse.

I dug my fingers under the cast on my arm, trying
to scratch the maddening itch while I watched Ryan
and my horse make tight serpentines back and forth
across the arena. She suddenly started trotting, and I
expected him to correct her, but then realized he must
have told her to do it. It was a slow trot, one he could
sit without bouncing too much, and as they came down
the rail toward me, the grin on his face was infectious.

I shook my head and laughed. All the cast and
broken bone bullshit aside, was there anything sexier
than a gorgeous man on a horse? Sweet fucking Christ.
Right then I decided that if I had to give up an entire
summer of riding, there were worse alternatives than
spending that summer watching Ryan ride.

Because *damn.*

CHAPTER SIX

By the time Tsarina was happily back in her stall and awaiting her evening feeding, my leg hurt like hell. Both of them did, actually. My left hip ached from lugging that stupid heavy cast around, plus not being properly elevated since I'd left my apartment, and every joint and muscle on the right side was sore from bearing my weight.

Needless to say, I wasn't moving very quickly.

It was worth it, though. Well worth it. Tsarina had been ridden, Ryan had had a chance to get back in the saddle, and I'd gotten about forty-five minutes' worth of eye candy. Not a bad evening.

On the way out of the barn, in spite of my sore legs, I didn't have to struggle to keep up with Ryan. He slowed down and adapted his pace to mine; just a little act of consideration, but I appreciated it more than he could have known. Asking people for even the slightest things like that bothered me, but with him I didn't have to. He just… did it.

He helped me into the truck, and I caught myself feeling a little disappointed that the afternoon was about to be over. It was hard to believe this was the same man I'd punched in a moment of fury the other day; I rather liked his company now.

"Do you, um…." I paused. "Do you want to get a drink or something?"

"I… uh…."

"Just, you know, thanks for working my horse for me," I said quickly. "Not a date or anything."

"Oh." His posture deflated a little, like my explanation had disappointed rather than reassured him.

It… could be a date? But I kept that to myself.

"I'll buy," I said. "It's about dinnertime anyway, right?"

He nodded. "It is. You sure? I can pay my way."

"I insist."

"Sure." We exchanged smiles, and he put the truck in gear.

Everyone else apparently had the same idea about grabbing dinner right then. Almost every restaurant's parking lot was packed, though we did finally stumble across a halfway decent diner just off the interstate. Probably not Michelin-starred fine dining, but it didn't seem like a place we might contract salmonella just by reading the menu.

A cheerful hostess greeted us. "Two tonight?"

"Yes, and would it be possible to get a booth?" Ryan gestured at me. "So he can put his leg up?"

"Oh, sure. Come with me."

It hadn't occurred to me to get a booth so I could prop up my leg. Thinking with my stomach instead of my broken bones, apparently, but at least one of us was on top of things.

Ryan slid into the booth opposite me, and he gently pulled my cast up so my foot rested on the bench beside him. "Comfortable?"

"As comfortable as this thing ever is."

"How's the pain?"

"Present and accounted for."

He grimaced. "You okay?"

I nodded and waved my uninjured hand. "It's fine. Beats sitting at home waiting for the walls to cave in on me."

"I can imagine," he said, and I thought he shuddered.

While he perused the menu, he absently ran his thumb along the perfectly trimmed edge of his goatee, and I caught myself imagining him shaving. Everything from carefully navigating the goatee's edge to dabbing away excess foam when he was done. Maybe in reality he used an electric razor, but not in my mind. White foam and a blade or I didn't want to know about it.

The waitress appeared beside our table, snapping me out of my foamy little fantasy. "What can I get you guys?"

Ryan looked at me, eyebrows up.

"Uh…." I glanced at the menu. "You go ahead. By the time you order, I'll know what I want."

He ordered, and I made an unusually fast decision to settle on the Reuben sandwich with a side of fries.

After the waitress had gone again, I said, "So it seems like you're pretty natural on the horse. Most people are wobbling all over the place the first time. Not that it was your *first* time, but you said it's been a while."

"I'm a fast learner," he said with a smile. "It's not that much different than a motorcycle, though. At least when it comes to balance."

"Hmm, I guess." I paused. "You ever thought about getting one? Or do you just want to learn for the hell of it?"

"I've thought about it, but…." Shrugging, he lowered his gaze and played with the edge of his place mat. "I don't stay in one place very long, so it's never really been practical."

"You don't stay in one place very long?"

Ryan shook his head. "No. I'm kind of a drifter, I guess."

"Really? So, what? You just go wherever the wind takes you?"

"Sort of. Sometimes I'll go someplace to work for someone who's offered me a job." He sat back, twisting a little as if to work out some stiffness in his back. "Stayed with my grandma for a year because she needed someone to work around the house. But sometimes, yeah, I'll pack up, pick a direction, and see where I end up."

"Oh. Interesting."

"I think I was born to be nomadic. Definitely raised that way."

"How do you mean?"

Ryan leaned forward again, resting his arm on the edge of the table. "My dad and stepdad were both career military. Every three or four years they moved, and they were staggered, so it seemed like one side or the other was always moving." He sighed as if just thinking about his childhood exhausted him. "I guess I never really got used to staying in one place for very long."

"I'm surprised you didn't enlist yourself," I said. "Seems like people get used to that life, and if they don't want to get as far from it as possible, they stay in it."

Ryan wrinkled his nose. "Nah. The military's not for me. I mean, I don't mind wandering around, but I like doing it on my terms. If I don't like something, I can move on."

"I guess that… that kind of makes sense. So, um, how long have you been in Tucker Springs?" *And how long do you plan to stay?*

"About six months. And then my uncle in Tucson's got a job for me starting the first part of November, so I'll be out of here before winter."

Guess that answered that. I ignored the pang of disappointment as much as I could, but it slipped into my voice as I said, "Oh. So just a few more months, then."

Ryan nodded. "Yep. Then we'll see how I like Arizona. If I don't, there's plenty of places I haven't been to yet."

Had it been anyone else, I would have thought that was a sad, lonely life. But Ryan seemed genuinely content with it. I couldn't comprehend that myself—the thought of moving into a new apartment within the same town was enough to make me hyperventilate—but obviously it worked for him.

And with that knowledge, a weird feeling twisted in the pit of my stomach as I sat across from him, curling the corner of my napkin around my finger. On the one hand, disappointment because he'd only be here a little longer. On the other, something… else. Something I couldn't quite identify. Like he'd just changed the rules, and now I was tempted to play.

Easy, Nathan. You don't even know if the man bats for your team.

I cleared my throat. "What was that like, always being on the move as a kid?"

"I don't have anything to compare it to." He shrugged. "It's all I ever knew. Some people assume it was hell, but it really wasn't. I wasn't miserable as a kid. I was happy. Just… kind of nomadic, I guess. I was a loner, not lonely."

"You still a loner?"

"Kind of. I have friends scattered here and there, and family of course." He paused for a sip of ice water, and he watched the ice cubes clinking against the inside of the glass as he spoke again. "Mostly, I like being on my own, and I'm used to moving around. About the only thing I ever commit to for any length of time is a tattoo."

My eyes darted toward the lines and colors sticking out from under his sleeve. "What is your tattoo, anyway?"

He pulled up his sleeve, revealing the entire design, which was a finely detailed bald eagle.

"Wow, that is some really nice work."

"Thanks." He smiled shyly and pulled the sleeve back down as the waitress arrived with his soda and my coffee. After she'd gone again, he asked, "You have any ink?"

"Not yet. I've been thinking about getting one."

"You should." He grinned. "They're addictive, though. I only meant to get one, but now I've got two and want to get a third."

"You have another one?"

Ryan nodded and gestured at the back of his right shoulder. "Nothing special. It's an Army emblem, since I was an Army brat." His grin turned to a playful smirk. "I'd show it to you, but I don't generally rip off my shirt in public." With a wink, he added, "Maybe when we get back to your place."

I blinked.

The mischievousness in his expression immediately changed to something more characteristically shy. He coughed and lowered his gaze to the place mat in front of him. "I've been meaning to get it redone anyway, actually. But, yeah, tattoos are addictive as hell."

"So I've heard." My mouth had gone dry, so I reached for my drink. "A friend of mine runs Ink Springs over in the Light District, and he's been trying to get me to come in and get one for like two years now."

Ryan met my eyes again. "Why don't you?"

"I might. Most of my disposable income has been going toward college or saving to buy Tsarina." I idly stirred my coffee. "Though now that I've bought her and have enough to care for her through the winter, and I'm not buying books until next semester...." I shrugged.

"Books?" He raised his eyebrows and leaned forward, folding his arms on the edge of the table. "So you're still in college?"

I nodded.

"What are you studying?"

"How to break my mother's heart, apparently."

He cocked his head. "What do you mean?"

"She's convinced any degree that doesn't involve law, medicine, computers, or business is going to land me a job at a drive-thru."

"Depends on what you want to do with it, right?" He folded his hands on the table. "What *do* you want to do with it? And what field is it, anyway?"

"History," I said.

His eyes lit up. "Yeah?"

I nodded. "Don't know how far it'll get me, but it's a degree."

"You studying any particular era?"

"American, post-European discovery."

Ryan grinned again. "A man after my own heart."

Maybe not your heart, but quite possibly some other things if you play your cards right. "Oh, really?"

He nodded. "My dad's into history. He has hundreds of books on it, and I started eating them up when I was a kid."

"Same here." I chuckled. "My teachers hated the fact that I read so damned much."

"Yours too?" Ryan shook his head, grinning mischievously. "Guess they didn't like us learning enough to argue with them."

"Yes." I smacked my palm on the table beside my coffee cup. "Exactly. You did that too?"

"All the fucking time. I once got detention in seventh grade for insisting that the Boston Tea Party was an act of economic terrorism."

"Oh yeah?" I folded my hands—well, put my uninjured hand over the top of the cast—and leaned forward. "I can do you one better than that."

"Let's hear it."

"So my sophomore year in high school, we were talking about the War of 1812…."

The coffee got cold. The food that eventually arrived mostly went untouched. Truth be told, I forgot there was food on the table at all until Ryan made an animated gesture during one story and almost knocked his soda into his lap.

By eight thirty, the waitresses were giving us dirty looks, so I paid the bill and we headed out. In the parking lot, Ryan started the truck, but he didn't put it in gear. "As long as you're out of the apartment, do you need to do anything else? Stock the refrigerator or anything?"

I was still a bit sore from being up and around earlier. Going home and relaxing was probably the best thing for me right now. And a pain pill. God, yes, a pain pill.

On the other hand, running a couple of errands was an excuse to put off facing those six flights of stairs for a little while. I also didn't want to impose on Brad, especially since he'd already insisted on buying far too many groceries for me to ask him to make this week's run. And we *were* already out and about. And though I needed to put up my leg and throw back a pain pill, for some reason I wasn't quite ready to go home yet.

"I could probably stand to grab a few groceries. Are you sure you don't mind?"

"Not at all." He put the truck in Reverse and rested his hand across the back of my seat as he backed out of the space. "Any particular grocery store preference?"

"Nah. I'm easy."

Ryan glanced at me, an eyebrow raised in *Did you really just say that?* fashion.

I groaned. "You know what I mean."

Chuckling, he shifted gears again.

"Very funny," I muttered. "So is this all part of your secret plan to keep me from suing you?"

Ryan grinned. "Is it working?"

"Well, I wasn't *planning* to sue you, but if it means having you chauffeur me around, I could always *tell* you I'm going to."

He laughed. "You would, wouldn't you?"

"Maybe."

We exchanged playful glances, and he kept driving.

"Hmm." I leaned on my crutch and glared at the plastic bags sitting in the truck bed. "This could get... complicated."

"Nah, it'll be fine." Ryan shut the driver's side door and came around to my side. "Why don't I help you get up to your apartment, and then I can come downstairs and get the bags?"

"Are you sure? I don't want you making a million trips to—"

"Don't worry about it. You need help getting to the top, and I can get all of that"—he gestured at the bags—"in one more trip. And yes, I'm sure."

I didn't protest. I thanked him quietly, plastered on a smile, and let him put his arm around my waist, pretending I didn't get goose bumps just from his hand sliding over the back of my shirt. Okay, so leaning on someone in any way was about as pleasant as jamming bamboo splinters under my toenails, but having an excuse to go hands-on with Ryan took some of the sting out.

Getting to the top of the stairs was, yet again, an exercise in undignified stumbling and swearing. Eventually I'd probably have to navigate them myself, but at least for tonight, I had Ryan to help me—*oh God, those shoulders*—so I didn't break my neck.

Once Ryan had helped me to the couch and I was getting myself situated with pillows and such, he left to get the groceries out of the truck. He returned just as I'd finally gotten myself comfortable.

"Doing okay?" he asked, toeing the door shut as he balanced the bags on his arms.

"Yeah, as long as I don't have to move anytime soon."

He laughed. "You're fine where you are. I'll put these away for you."

"You sure? Brad will be home shortly, so I could have him do it."

"Brad?" Ryan stopped in his tracks and raised his eyebrows. "Your…?"

"Roommate," I said.

"Oh."

I waved a hand. "Not my boyfriend, if that's what you were thinking. I haven't had one of those in a while."

Ryan laughed. "Neither have I."

Aha. So he is gay.

Right. Because the lingering eye contact over dinner and the excuse to stay out a little longer hadn't been a goddamned clue.

"Well. Um. Anyway." I cleared my throat and gestured toward the kitchen. "Just leave everything on the counter."

"Really? It'll only take a minute."

I hesitated, but then shrugged. "It's up to you. I don't want to work you into the ground or something."

"Don't worry about it." He continued toward the kitchen. "I'll take care of it. Won't take a minute."

In the kitchen, plastic bags rustled. The pantry and refrigerator doors opened and closed. I was almost embarrassingly obsessive about where everything was stored, but I forced myself to take a few deep breaths and not worry about it. Ryan was doing me a massive favor. The Wheat Thins would not be rendered inedible if they ended up on the second pantry shelf instead of the third, and I would not break out in hives if a soup can wasn't turned label out.

A few minutes later he came out of the kitchen. "That should hold you for a little while, I think."

"Thanks. I really appreciate it."

"Don't mention it." He glanced at the clock on the DVD player. "I should really get going, though. It's an early morning for me."

"Oh shit. I hope I didn't keep you out too late."

"Nah, you're fine. But I'd better roll out. Do you, um, need anything before I go?" He pointed over his shoulder with his thumb. "From the kitchen or anything?"

"No, I'll be okay. Brad will be home pretty soon." I paused. "And, um, thanks again. For everything. Especially what you're doing with Tsarina. It's... it's a big help."

"Don't mention it. I'm happy to help."

"Well, thanks."

"You're welcome." He took out his truck keys and spun them on his finger. "And thanks for dinner."

"You're welcome." I smiled. "I enjoyed the company."

"Me too."

Silence tried to set in. I was about to say something to fill the void, but Ryan beat me to it.

"Do you, um, want to get something to eat tomorrow night?" His cheeks darkened slightly. "I mean, to get out of the apartment? Not a date?"

But can *it be a date?* "Sure. You want to ride again?"

"Yes, definitely."

"Great." I paused. "And actually, I'm going back to work tomorrow. I work in town, in the Light District. If it's easier for you, we can meet there instead of having you come all the way out here."

"Whatever's easiest for you." He kept playing with his truck keys. "My apartment's not far from the Light District. I'll need to grab a shower after work, but then I can come pick you up." He lifted his gaze and met my eyes.

"I'm off at five."

Ryan smiled. "I'll see you then. Text me the address?"

"Will do."

"Great." He glanced at the door. "So, um, I'd better go. Do you want me to lock it on my way out?"

"Don't worry about it. This building's safe enough."

He nodded once. "Okay. Well, I'll see you tomorrow. Good night."

"Good night."

After the front door clicked shut behind him, I closed my eyes and rested my head against the pillow. I was suddenly exhausted. My body had been dragging for the past few hours, but I'd kept finding a second, third, fourth wind because I just hadn't been ready to come home. Dinner? Hell, why not? Wander through the grocery store? Sure.

Of course that meant it had to catch up with me at some point. The aching was relentless, and it was everywhere. My head was pounding the way it did after I pulled an all-nighter before a big exam. A pain pill would knock me the rest of the way out. And I'd take one. In a minute. First I wanted to… sit here. And not move. At all.

I was starting to drift off when the front door opened. Blinking sleepily, I turned my head, and the instant I saw Brad, I was wide-awake. He looked more exhausted than I was.

"Rough night?" I asked.

"You could say that." He gestured at the kitchen. "I'm going to grab a beer. You want anything?"

"No, thanks."

Once he had a beer in hand, he came back in and dropped onto the recliner.

"That bad, huh?"

He rolled his eyes and grumbled something under his breath. Well, it was no mystery where he'd been so late, then. Brad coming home at this hour in a pissy mood meant one thing and one thing only.

"So did you guys *get* anywhere this time?" I hoped I wasn't prodding a raw nerve. "Progress one way or another?"

"Ehhh...."

"That sounds like a no."

"Kind of. We.... God, I don't know what to do." He rubbed his forehead. "I am so sick of all the bullshit, but I'm not ready to let him go."

"Are you sure you're not just holding on because you want to be with *someone*?" I asked. "Or maybe because you guys had something so good in the beginning, you don't want to let go even though that part is over?"

Brad shook his head. "I don't know. Sometimes I think we're doing CPR on a corpse. Sometimes I think if we work at it for a *little* while longer, we can bring it back to life."

"Assuming you don't kill yourselves—or each other—in the process."

He grunted into his beer bottle before taking a long drink. "I talked to my mom last night too. And she reminded me that if I love Jeff, I should let him go. If he comes back...." He sighed. "You know the rest."

I nodded. "Yeah, I do. She's right, though. If he doesn't come back, then, I mean, maybe once you both have some closure, you can move on, you know?"

"Yeah. Maybe. All I know right now is that I'm not ready to give up on him."

Though I couldn't help thinking they were both beating their heads against a brick wall, I had to admire them for putting this much effort into saving their relationship.

It sure didn't do much to convince me to jump back into the dating pool, though. I was all for getting laid once in a while—preferably more often than that— but not if the price was all this arguing and compromising and whatever nonsense. I hadn't had a boyfriend in almost a year now, not since I'd walked away from that cheating asshole who had an overactive gag reflex except when it came to longneck bottles or his roommate's dick. I was *over* that shit.

Brad rubbed his hand over his face. "Maybe we'll get somewhere eventually."

"Good luck." I wished I had a scrap of optimism for them. I certainly didn't envy them. The more I watched those two unravel, the more I ached for both of them and the less interested I was in getting involved with anyone myself.

It just wasn't worth it.

CHAPTER SEVEN

"ARE YOU sure you don't need help?" Brad stood in the kitchen doorway, fussing with his tie. "I can be a little late to work if—"

"I'll be fine." I glanced up from pouring myself another cup of coffee. "I'm going to be wearing these things for almost three months, and I'll have to get myself around sooner or later."

He scowled. "Yeah, but 'sooner' means you're probably still sore and getting used to moving around on flat ground." He stopped messing with his tie and folded his arms. "Doesn't seem like a good time to be tackling six flights of stairs on your own, you know?"

"I'll be *fine*. I'll just leave early and give myself time to get to the bottom without breaking my neck."

"If you were on two crutches, I'd say that was a good idea." He eyed the single crutch under my arm. "But with one? Dude, you are asking for it."

I glared at him.

He put up his hands and shrugged. "Your funeral."

Okay, so maybe he had a point. His point didn't trump my stubbornness, though, which was probably why he quit arguing. We'd been friends long enough, he knew when it wasn't worth it. A lesson I probably needed to learn myself, but whatever. I could do this, damn it.

I'd taken almost a week off work so I could swim in pain pill euphoria for a few days, and the cabin fever had officially become unbearable. Time to get back to work. Plus, I was bound and determined to leave this apartment and get around on my own. No way in hell was I relying on other people to cart me around, especially up and down the goddamned stairs, because that would turn my apartment—my sanctuary of independence—into my own personal Alcatraz.

So not long after Brad left for work, I headed out myself.

I stopped at the top of the stairs.

My nemesis. We meet again.

One step at a time. I could do this. Using the crutch like a cane and resting my cast hand on the railing, I gingerly took the first step. Cast first. Good leg second. Then again. Same slow process, over and over, but eventually I made it. As my foot touched down on the landing, I grinned. No way in hell was a flight of motherfucking stairs making me its bitch.

Leaning on the crutch, I turned the corner.

My grin fell. My heart slowly sank all the way into my feet.

One flight of stairs might not make me its bitch. It was the remaining five that could be a problem.

I inched closer to the top step. Then I took a deep breath, adjusted my crutch, and started down. By the time I made it to the next landing, I was sweating. Just four more and I could relax in the car. And my job kept me at a desk most of the day—plus Mike would probably forbid me from moving around much once he saw me like this—so all I had to do was get past these damned stairs, and it was all downhill from there. So to speak.

Slowly, steadily, I made it down the third flight. At the top of the fourth, my right leg started seizing up from my hip all the way to my calf, fatigue and the stress of doing the work of two legs stiffening it until it wasn't much more flexible than the cast around the left.

I gritted my teeth. No one had ever said this would be a pleasant process. I'd come this far; I could make it the rest of the way.

I started down the fourth flight.

After two steps my right knee buckled. I dropped my crutch and grabbed the railing, which stopped me from falling, but I was helpless to keep the crutch from clattering the rest of the way down. It came to a stop with the shoulder pad on the very last step and the rest of the crutch extending across the landing in a crude display of what I would be doing if I didn't successfully navigate these steps.

Heart pounding and joints screaming, I swore under my breath and eased myself down onto the third step.

Okay. This wasn't going to work.

Halfway down was also halfway up. Three flights to go in either direction. Up would have been the easier option—*Mike, I think I need a few more days off; is that okay?*—if I hadn't exhausted my uninjured leg fighting my way this far down. Now both directions were equally daunting. No two ways about it: I wasn't doing this alone. Not today.

Sighing, I pulled out my cell phone and glared at it. When it came to asking for help, I was like a straight man asking for directions. Pride wouldn't get me up or down these stairs, though, so I grudgingly scrolled through my contacts.

He's at work. She's an hour away. He'd never let me hear the end of it. She's got the kids this week. What the hell is this *dickhole still doing in my phone?*

And then, like a contact straight from the man upstairs himself: Owen.

I speed-dialed him and hoped he hadn't left it on silent like he sometimes did when he was working. Or left it in his car or someplace where he wouldn't hear it.

"Hey, Nathan," he said. "What's up?"

"Hey. Um, are you busy right now?"

A chair creaked. Probably his desk chair. Shit, that meant he was busy. "I've got a lot of work today. Why?"

"Uh. I...." I sighed. "Don't worry about it. I can—"

"Nathan. Do you need something?"

I chewed the inside of my cheek. I reached up to rub my eyes, but the cast on my hand stopped me, and also reminded me why I was calling Owen in the first place. "I, um, I hate to ask, but I could really use a hand right now."

He was silent for a moment. "A hand? Really?"

I winced. Of all the people I could have used that expression on.... "Sorry. That's... fuck. I'm sorry."

Owen laughed. "It's all right." The chair creaked again and a set of keys jingled. "Where are you?"

"At my apartment." *Well, sort of.*

"I'll be right there."

After we'd hung up, I set the phone on the step beside me and tried to get comfortable. I was starting to realize why the good doctor had suggested keeping my leg elevated as much as possible. Maybe it was the debacle of getting down the stairs or the fact that I'd overdone it yesterday, but my leg was starting to throb like a motherfucker. I kneaded my thigh above the cast, hoping it would relieve at least some of the fatigue.

Sitting up here, I must have looked like a complete jackass.

This will be fun to explain to Owen.

It occurred to me right then that he had no idea what was going on. All the information he had was that I needed help—a hand, because I was so damned tactful—and was at my apartment. He hadn't asked for anything further, just said he'd be right over. Good guy, that one. In fact, his boyfriend and I had decided one night that since Owen didn't seem to have a jerk bone in his body, the jerk bone in the rest of us must have been located somewhere in the lower left arm, which Owen was missing.

The thought made me chuckle. It was true, though. He was a great guy, and thank God he didn't live far from here.

Maybe ten minutes after I'd made the call, the stairwell door opened a floor and a half below me. Must've been one of my neighbors. I cringed, hoping they lived on the second floor and wouldn't make it far enough to see me sitting here like an idiot. Judging by the rapid, almost jogging steps, they were in a hurry, so maybe there wouldn't be time for the otherwise inevitable awkward questions.

I braced myself as the person came around the corner below me, and—

"Wow." My jaw dropped. "How fast did you drive?"

Owen shrugged. "Hey, when Mr. Independence says he needs help, it's worth risking a speeding ticket or two." He leaned down to pick up my crutch, then eyed me. "So, what in the world…?"

"It's a long story." I held out my hand. Owen came up the stairs and gave me the crutch. Using it as, well, a crutch, I started to ease myself upward.

Owen took my arm and helped me the rest of the way to my feet. "So were you on your way up or down?"

"Down." I scowled. "I'm supposed to be heading back to work today."

His forehead creased. "You sure you should be going to work instead of resting?"

"Not really, but I need to." I pointed at the ceiling. "Gotta pay rent on the castle in the clouds."

"Yeah, but if you hurt yourself again, you're going to have to take more time off."

"Hey." I made a not-very-menacing gesture with my cast. "You keep your logic to yourself, buster."

Owen laughed. "All right, all right. Let's get you downstairs." He paused. "Hmm. So we're down a leg and two arms between us." He smirked. "This could get interesting."

"Yeah. Something like that." I thought for a moment. "Okay. I think I know how we can do this."

"I'm all ears."

"If I put my left arm around your shoulders, then I can grab the railing with my other."

"And if we lose our balance…?"

"Fuck."

Through a fair amount of trial and error, not to mention alternately swearing in frustration and laughing at the ridiculousness of the situation, we got our respective limbs in order, and by the grace of God, we made it to the ground floor without incident. There was a bench right outside, and Owen guided me to it and helped me sit.

"You know," I said as I struggled to catch my breath, "one of the reasons I rented this place was I figured going up and down the stairs would keep me from getting lazy. Didn't that come back and bite me in the ass?"

He laughed. "The universe has a hell of a sense of humor sometimes."

"Yeah, it does."

"So are you going to tell me what happened, or what?"

I told him the story. When I'd finished, he whistled. "Wow. Sounds like you got lucky."

I laughed dryly. "I don't know if that's the word I'd use, but yeah, it could've been worse."

"A lot worse." He pulled out his keys and gestured at his car. "As long as I'm here, do you need a lift?"

I shook my head. "My left leg's the one that's jacked up, so I can still drive."

"Nathan." Owen rolled his eyes. "You know you're talking to someone who hates when people assume he needs help or can't do something just because of"—he gestured with his stump—"but if you push yourself too hard, you're going to take longer to heal."

"Driving isn't pushing myself too hard."

"No, but you might find at the end of the day that you're hurting enough that you don't want to, or you'll be too exhausted to drive safely."

Every bit of my trademark stubbornness wanted to scream that he was wrong, but... I definitely wasn't back to a hundred percent yet. If the stairs could kick my ass like this, then an eight-hour day in the clinic would probably have me whimpering and begging for mercy well before I clocked out.

I blew out a breath. "You really don't mind?"

"Of course not." He smiled. "Come on, cripple. Let's go."

He helped me up, and we got into his car. On the way into town, he said, "What about tonight? Do you want me to have Nick pick you up on his way home?"

I waved my hand. "No, that's okay. I'm supposed to be meeting up with someone after work, so I'll get a lift from him."

"Meeting someone?" Owen glanced at me and grinned. "Didn't know you were seeing anyone."

"I'm not seeing anyone. I'm teaching him to ride, and he's keeping my horse exercised while I'm...." I gestured at my useless limbs.

"I hope you're not teaching by example," he said.

"Oh, shut up." I rolled my eyes. "I'm damned good at riding when the horse actually, you know, stays on her feet."

Owen winced. "Minor detail, right?"

"Very. Because they usually do stay on their feet." I fidgeted a bit, trying to get comfortable. "But for the moment, I'm out of commission, and Ryan volunteered to keep Tsarina exercised in exchange for some lessons."

Owen eyed me. "And you're not seeing him."

"No. What makes you think I am?"

"Nothing." He shrugged and shook his head. "Nothing at all."

"Bullshit."

Chuckling, he glanced at me. "Okay, besides the fact that as soon as you mentioned him, you got that ridiculous grin on your face."

I was grinning, wasn't I? What the hell? I cleared my throat. "Yeah. Well. He's cute, but he's leaving the area in a few months anyway, so there isn't much point in getting involved with him."

Owen shrugged again. "Just means if you're going to do it, you'd better do it. Before he leaves."

"Even though I know he's going to leave?"

"Why not?" Owen smiled. "Could be fun while it lasts."

"And what about when it's over?"

His smile fell, and after a moment he nodded. "Okay. There is that."

"Exactly. I'll just stick to giving him riding lessons."

"Good plan."

When we arrived, Owen helped me out of the car and held the clinic's door open for me. "You need anything, give me a call. All right?"

"Will do. Thanks, man. I owe you one."

He shrugged. "Don't worry about it."

"I'll buy you a beer or something."

"Not going to turn that down."

"Deal."

He left, and I hobbled toward my desk.

To my great surprise, the paperwork hadn't piled up much in my absence. A few insurance claim forms, maybe half a day's worth of charts that needed to be filed. The work waiting for me was easily under 10 percent of what I'd anticipated.

"Oh my God." Mike's voice made me jump. When I turned around, he was staring at me with wide eyes.

"When you said you'd gotten dumped off the horse, I was thinking…. How fast were you *going*?" Before I could respond, though, he pointed at my chair. "Sit. I'll get you another to elevate that leg." And he disappeared down the hall.

He returned a moment later with a chair from the back and helped me get situated with my leg up on the chair with a pillow under it. I saw the question in his eyes and quickly diverted him: "So have you seen *any* patients since I've been gone?"

He cocked his head. "Of course I have. Why?"

"Because… my desk…."

"Your—" Then he nodded. "Oh, right. Jason came in and gave me a hand with the filing and everything. I hope that's okay."

"Okay? Dude, it's your operation here. But if he messed anything up, you'd better blame him and not me."

Mike laughed. "Don't worry. He's got a better handle on this sort of thing than I do."

I scowled. "You're not going to lay me off and hire him, are you?"

"Oh God, no." He groaned. "I love him with all my heart, but we'd kill each other. And besides, he still has the club to run." Then Mike's expression turned serious, and I knew exactly what was coming next: "So, what happened, exactly?"

I exhaled hard. "So I took Tsarina out on the trails…."

When I'd finished, Mike shook his head. "Wow. And how's your other leg doing?"

"It was fine until I tried to come down the stairs this morning." I shifted gingerly. "Now it hurts."

Mike glared at my leg as if it might offer up some explanation for its lack of cooperation. "Well, take it easy today. If the pain gets out of hand, you might need a little treatment on it. Just to keep the inflammation down."

"I'll let you know. Thanks."

Mike went back to check on a couple of patients, and I got to work. Since I was typing at a fraction of my normal speed, I made notes by hand. Of course, since I was writing with my left hand, those notes took a hell of a lot of effort to write. By ten thirty, my desk was covered in sticky notes that might as well have been written by a four-year-old.

And by noon, I was ready to never tell anyone what had happened ever again. The jingle of the bell on the front door made me cringe because invariably, the first thing out of any newcomer's mouth was "Oh my! What in the world happened to you?"

From there, the conversations proceeded predictably, nearly every one of them a variation of the same:

"Oh! Are you going to sue the guy? Damned reckless motorcyclists. You should file a complaint with the county for letting those bikes out on the same trails as horses. But anyway, sounds like you got lucky. My brother's wife's cousin's babysitter's ex-husband's psychic once had a dog sitter who fell off a horse and broke seventy-eight bones in her body. Paralyzed from the ears down too! And that horse was barely even *moving* when it happened!"

That, or the endless well-meaning but nevertheless frustrating offers to help me with everything. I appreciated people's generosity, but my God, I loathed being in that position.

I loathed it almost as much as I did this motherfucking itch. Holy shit. I dug my finger under the edge of the cast on my arm, clawing at the incessant irritation underneath it. Twenty-first goddamned century, and we still hadn't figured out how to put on a cast that wouldn't make the skin itch like this?

The phone rang again. Of course.

Somewhere in the middle of all the ringing phones and itching limbs and incomprehensible notes, my cell phone vibrated on my desk. *God. Now what?* The day had already spiraled into a trifecta of things I hated—sympathy, dependence, and inefficiency—and I still had a few hours to go. I didn't want to be bothered by—

Ryan.

Four letters on my caller ID, and half a day's worth of tension melted out of my shoulders.

"Hey," I said. "What's up?"

"This isn't a bad time, is it?"

"No, you're fine. Long as I'm getting stuff done, the boss man's easy on me."

"Good, good. I'll keep it short anyway. I just realized I still don't have the address where you work so I can come by tonight."

"Oh, shit, you're right. I'm sorry. I completely forgot to text you." I gave him the address and added, "Come down the main drag in the Light District and look for the sign for Ink Springs. The acupuncture clinic is right across the street."

"Sounds good. Five o'clock, right?"

"Five o'clock."

"I'll be there."

HE WAS right on time.

As he got out of the truck, I stole a glance at him and caught myself wondering if he wore a leather jacket when the weather was colder. He sure seemed like the type with those beat-up boots, the jeans with threadbare knees, and a Led Zeppelin T-shirt that was probably as old as he was. He had a little scruff on his jaw, a dusting of five-o'clock shadow, which of course looked great on him. What didn't?

He pulled open the clinic door and smiled as he took off his sunglasses. "Hey. How are you doing?"

"Not bad." I closed the chart I'd been working on. "Made it through the day."

"That's a plus." He scanned the waiting area, probably taking in the Chinese artwork, acupuncture diagrams, and some of the odd trinkets Mike had picked up when he'd visited China while he'd been studying.

Ryan's nose twitched like most people's did the first time they came in here. I'd long ago gotten used to the pungent herbal smell of the clinic, but a newcomer's reaction to it always reminded my senses that the scent was there.

I chuckled. "You get used to the smell."

"What is it?" he asked.

"Herbs and stuff. If you think they smell bad, try drinking them." I made a face.

He laughed. "I'll pass, but thanks."

"I don't blame you," I said in a stage whisper. "Okay, I think I'm about ready to go. Let me make sure the boss is—"

"The boss wants you to get out of here and take it easy." Mike came around the corner. "And if you need another day off, just say so, all right?"

"Okay, okay."

Mike extended his hand to Ryan. "I'm Dr. Whitman. You are…?"

"Ryan." He shook Mike's hand. "I, uh, kind of broke your receptionist."

Mike's eyebrows shot upward. "I beg your pardon?"

"He was the one on the motorcycle." I gingerly pushed myself up and put the crutch under my arm. "So he's riding Tsarina for me."

"He…." Mike glanced back and forth between us. Then he shrugged. "Okay. That sounds like an interesting arrangement."

"I'm not sure it makes us even." Ryan smiled sheepishly. "But if I can help keep Tsarina exercised and learn how to ride as part of the deal, I won't complain."

"It makes us even enough." I took a step and winced when pain reverberated up through my good leg. I'd been sitting most of the day, with occasional trips up and down the hallway to stretch and keep everything from seizing up. Still, after this morning's stairway-to-hell debacle and overdoing it last night, every goddamned joint hurt. The thought of getting from the clinic to Ryan's truck made my eyes water, and imagining myself getting from the truck to Tsarina's stall or to the bleachers was enough to nauseate me. Maybe I should have taken Mike up on his treatment offer after all.

"Hey." Mike put a gentle hand on my arm. "You all right?"

"I'm fine."

"You sure?" Ryan asked. "You seem a little pale."

"Yeah. Uh, listen." I sighed. "I hate to do this, but do you mind if we skip the lesson tonight?" I gestured at my leg. "This is the most I've been up and around, and—"

"Absolutely."

"Thanks. I'm sorry to have you come all the way out here for nothing."

He gave me an odd look. Part puzzled, part amused. But then he shrugged. "Well, as long as I'm out here, do you want to get something to eat, or a cup of coffee or something?"

"That actually sounds really good. I'll buy."

"Don't worry about it." He smiled. "We'll go Dutch."

"Dutch works."

He didn't need to know I had zero intention of letting him pick up his part of the bill.

CHAPTER EIGHT

WE FOUND a restaurant down by the river. It was one of those generic "family" joints with a little bit of everything, the kind of place with crayons for the kids and twelve local brews on tap for Mom and Dad.

The hostess took one look at my leg and said she'd find us a booth. I was too tired to feel like an imposition or an invalid, so I just smiled and thanked her.

Ryan helped me put my foot up, and the hostess left us with a couple of menus. While we read over the options, he asked, "So how was it, being back at work?"

"Not bad, but definitely tiring."

He grimaced. "I can imagine."

"The worst part, though?" I rolled my eyes. "The questions."

"The questions?"

I nodded. "Every single person asked what happened. Which, okay, I get it, but after the thirtieth time?"

"Oh God, I think I would have lost my mind."

"I almost did. Especially since everyone turns into a medical and legal expert." I shook my head. "As if getting around like this isn't hard enough without the constant commentary from self-proclaimed experts."

Ryan flinched. "God, I am so sorry about all this."

I straightened. "What? No. No, it's not...." Okay, so technically he *had* played a pretty significant part in all of this. But it occurred to me then that all day long, when I'd been ready to go on a hobbling rampage and beat a few people with my crutch, my frustration had never been directed at him. In fact, hadn't it been his name on the caller ID that had grounded me and brought back some of my sanity?

"Listen," I said. "I told you last night, and I still mean it: this wasn't your fault. What happened, it was an accident. And people totally mean well, I...." I sighed. "Let's put it this way: if I have to explain what happened to one more person...."

"Why explain it?" Ryan grinned mischievously. "Make something up."

"Make some— Really?"

"Why not?" The grin turned a bit more devilish. "Bar brawl? Bungee-jumping mishap?"

I laughed. "A bungee-jumping mishap. That's a good one."

"See?" Ryan winked. "Just because they ask doesn't mean you have to tell them the truth."

"I hadn't thought of that. You like fucking with people, don't you?"

Chuckling, he half shrugged. "A little harmless fun like that never hurt anybody."

"True, I suppose it hasn't."

A moment later a flustered brunette appeared beside us with a notepad in hand. "Sorry for the wait, guys."

"It's okay," Ryan said with a smile that probably weakened her knees. God knew it had that effect on me. "We're not in any hurry."

"Okay, well, what can I get you to start off? Something to drink or—" She glanced down and her eyes widened. "Oh, honey! What happened to your leg?"

I suppressed a groan. Not again.

"Oh, that was my fault," Ryan said. "Spent six months trying to talk him into going bungee jumping, he finally goes, and...." He gestured at my foot on the bench beside him.

The waitress blinked. "Bungee jumping?"

I clicked my tongue and nodded. "Trust this guy to sign us up with a discount fly-by-night place."

"They seemed legit."

"Their logo was spray-painted on their van!"

The waitress laughed. "And you still did it?"

I shrugged. "I'd already paid my deposit. Figured, eh, what could go wrong?" I threw Ryan a playful glare.

He put up his hands. "I never claimed to be an expert on these things!"

The waitress laughed again, shaking her head. "I don't even want to know. So can I get you boys something to drink?"

Ryan glanced at the back of his menu. "Will I get chased out of town for ordering a nonlocal beer?"

"I'll put it in a glass so no one notices," she said in a stage whisper.

"Awesome. I'll take a Bud Light."

She wrote it down and asked me, "For you?"

"I'll have the same."

"Thought you weren't supposed to be drinking," Ryan said.

"I haven't taken a painkiller all day. I'll be fine."

"Well," the waitress said, "I *will* have to see your ID."

I sighed with mock indignation as I pulled out my wallet. "Only me? Not him?"

Ryan smirked as he emphatically stroked his goatee. "Can't help it if I look my age."

"Mm-hmm." I handed my driver's license to the waitress.

Once she was satisfied I was in fact over twenty-one, she handed it back. Then she turned to Ryan and held out her hand. "Just to be on the safe side."

Ryan pulled out his wallet and handed over his license.

"Oh." Her eyebrows rose. "And here I thought he was the younger one."

"What?" I peered at the license in her hand. "No way."

She gave it to me, and sure enough, Ryan was younger.

"Eh, I've only got six months on you." I slid his driver's license back across the table. "I suppose I can live with that."

The waitress laughed. "Well, I'll get you boys your drinks while you go over the menus. And no bungee jumping while I'm gone, okay?"

As she walked away, Ryan flashed me a devilish grin. "See? You don't *have* to tell everyone the truth." He gestured at our waitress. "It gave her a laugh too, so...."

"Fair point, fair point."

We perused the menus for a minute, and when the waitress returned with our beers, we ordered dinner.

Ryan took a drink, and as he set the glass on the table, he said, "So out of curiosity, how did you end up working in an acupuncture clinic?"

"The short answer? I'd had enough of delivering pizzas."

"Oh yeah. I can't blame you. That's a shit job."

"You've done it?"

He nodded. "Unfortunately. But how did you get from pizza to acupuncture?"

Thumbing the edge of my menu, I said, "The clinic used to be in this strip mall on the other side of town. I was delivering pizzas to one of the offices a couple doors down, and I happened to see the Help Wanted sign in his window. Stopped in, asked for an application, and… here I am. When he moved over to the Light District, it meant a longer commute, but I love working for Mike, so I went with him."

"So you really like the job?"

"Oh yeah. Mike's awesome, and it's a pretty low-stress gig." I shrugged. "I can't complain. And it has its interesting moments."

"Does it?"

I nodded. "He usually helps people with things like chronic pain and allergies, but he does a *lot* of infertility work too." I smirked. "I'll tell you, it was a little weird the first time someone came in to thank him for getting her pregnant."

Ryan laughed. "Oh, wow, yeah. I can imagine."

"And while we're on the subject of jobs," I said. "I never did ask what you do."

"A little of everything. Right now I'm working in a mechanic's shop down by Tucker University. Nothing all that glamorous."

"Pays the bills, right?"

He nodded. "That it does. Which is good, because the cost of living here...." He whistled and shook his head.

"Is it really that bad compared to other places?"

"Compared to some places, yeah."

"Guess you'd know better than I would." I paused. "I have to admit, I'm still curious about what it's like to move around as much as you do."

"What do you want to know?"

"I'm, um, not sure. It's just the polar opposite of what I grew up with. I mean, don't you miss people when you move?"

"Sometimes. I don't—"

He paused when the waitress returned with a basket of rolls. Ryan took one and then smirked at me. "Do you, uh, need a hand?"

"No, I most certainly do not." I pulled a roll out of the basket, at which point it dawned on me that buttering said roll was a two-handed operation. Guess I was eating it without butter. "Anyway, you were saying? About missing people when you move?"

"Oh, right." He shrugged. "I don't tend to make a lot of friends wherever I go. I'm usually only there for a few months, maybe a year, and I'm...." He lowered his gaze, some color blooming in his cheeks. "I've never been that great at meeting people."

"Really?"

"Really. Once in a while I'll make friends at work, but beyond that, I've never been good at it." He tore open the roll in his hand and sliced off a pat of butter from the plate next to the basket. As he buttered the roll, he went on. "I'm not really sure how to meet people, to be honest." He laughed softly, almost cautiously. "Besides crashing into them, anyway."

"You know, I'm pretty sure I've never seen that in any self-help guide to meeting people."

"Maybe I should write one. *How to Make an Impression, Broken Bones and All.*"

I choked on my beer.

Ryan laughed. "Sorry."

I coughed a couple of times. "Well, I'm pretty sure there aren't any other books out there like that one."

"Yeah, there's probably a reason for that."

"Hmm, maybe." I paused. "But I will say the technique worked okay this time."

He raised his eyebrows, then laughed again as he laid the butter knife on the edge of the plate. "Yeah, it did. Probably the only way I ever would have worked up the nerve to say anything to you."

"And to think"—I held up my casted hand—"I almost blew it."

"Nah." Shaking his head, Ryan laughed with a bit more confidence this time. "I'm pretty sure I deserved that."

Our eyes met. I couldn't decide if the awkwardness stemmed from the discussion of how we met or the fact that we were gazing at each other like two guys who weren't just here because of a postaccident arrangement. Wherever it came from, it needed to go. Stat.

I cleared my throat. "So, is it just you? Or do you have brothers and sisters?"

"I have an older sister." He smiled fondly. "She's the exact opposite of me, though." He took a bite of the roll, and after he'd washed it down with another swig of beer, continued. "As soon as she moved out of Mom's house, she was ready to put down roots. She bought a house when she was twenty-one, and I doubt she'll ever move out of it without one hell of a good reason." He played with the coaster under his beer glass. "Me? I get restless. I'm so used to picking up and moving every eighteen months or so, I start feeling fenced in if I stick around for more than a couple of years."

"And it really doesn't get...."

"Lonely?"

I nodded.

Ryan shrugged. "I do okay on my own. I've always been like that. As long as I've got a working engine and a road in front of me, I'm happy."

"Do you ever go back to places you've been?"

Another shrug. "Sometimes. I stop in and see family in a few places. Couple of friends here and there. Other places, I'll pass through again on my way somewhere else. Visit people if there's anyone there who I've kept in touch with, keep going if there isn't."

"How did you end up in Tucker Springs?"

"Uh, well...." Laughing quietly, he blushed.

"What?"

"Um." Ryan looked at me through his lashes. "I decided I wanted to live here after I visited with some buddies last summer." He smiled sheepishly. "To do some dirt-biking."

I laughed. "Guess that makes sense, doesn't it?"

"Yeah." He took a drink, and for a moment we both nibbled our rolls and drank our beer. "So what about you? What brought you to this place?"

"I was born and raised here."

"Really? You've been here... your whole life?"

I nodded. "I mean, I've traveled, but I've never lived anywhere else."

"Wow. I guess that's not that unusual, but for me, it's about as hard to imagine as my life probably is for you."

"You're probably right."

"So does your family still live around here?"

"My sister lives in Denver and my brother's in Fort Collins, but our parents moved to Florida a few years ago. Dad decided he'd been through enough blizzards for a lifetime." I rolled my eyes. "And now he complains about the mosquitoes."

Ryan laughed. "There's always something."

"What about your parents? Do they still move around?"

"Not really. My mom and stepdad moved back to my mom's hometown to be close to my grandparents. My dad got remarried right after he retired, and I don't think my stepmom wants to move."

"Can you blame them?"

He shrugged. "No. I'll probably get tired of it eventually too."

"So what about the places you've lived? Ever live out of the country?"

Ryan nodded. "My dad spent two years in Germany when I was in elementary school, and my mom spent two in Guam right before I graduated high school."

"Guam?" I leaned a little closer. "What was that like?"

"How LONG do you think it'll be before every server in town groans when they see us coming?"

Ryan laughed as we started up the next flight of stairs to my apartment. "Hey, we tip well. I'm sure that makes up for occupying a table for three and a half hours."

"I hope so." I grimaced on the way up another step.

"And if that doesn't help, we probably entertain them when they catch snippets of our conversations."

I laughed. "Yeah, true. Though I still think you're full of shit with that story about the birds on Guam."

"I swear to God, it's true." He paused to adjust his arm around my waist. "No bullshit."

"Uh-huh." I eyed him as we cleared another step. "All the guys on base wear fake snakes around their necks when they jog."

"Yep."

"And if they don't, the birds really dive-bomb them?"

"I've never seen it happen, but everyone on the island swore it was true."

I gave him another skeptical look. "Mm-hmm."

"Google it!"

"I think I may have to, because that sounds about as believable as me breaking my leg in a bungee-jumping mishap."

Ryan just laughed.

At the top of the stairs, he let me go and handed back my crutch.

I pulled my keys out of my pocket. "Thanks again."

"You're welcome." That shy smile materialized again. "And even without going to the barn, I still had a great time."

"Yeah, me too." I couldn't look away from him. God, he was gorgeous, and in spite of his shyness, he stared right back at me. The moment lingered, and I didn't know what to make of this or of him, but finally I broke eye contact. "So, um, when do you want to try for another lesson?"

"Whenever you're up to it. I'm free most evenings."

"I don't want to waste your time, though. Commit to a lesson and then have to bail."

"Well, we can plan for, say, tomorrow night," he said. "And if you're not up to it, we'll find another restaurant to haunt until closing time."

I held his gaze for a moment, not sure what to say to that.

He lowered his chin a little, eyebrows up as he waited for my answer.

"Um…." I paused to collect my thoughts and clear my throat. "Come by the clinic at five?"

The inquisitive expression shifted to a satisfied smile. "I'll be there."

"Great. I'll see you then."

"See you then. Good night, Nathan."

"Good night."

CHAPTER NINE

ON THE way out of the clinic a few evenings later, Ryan glanced across the street at Ink Springs. "You said you know the guy who runs that place, right?"

I nodded. "Yeah. He's a friend of mine."

"He any good?" Ryan turned to me. "I mean, his work? Is it good?"

"Oh yeah. He's one of the better ones in Tucker Springs." I gestured toward the shop. "You want to check out his designs?"

Ryan hesitated but then nodded. "Why not? I'm sure Tsarina can handle being neglected for another ten minutes."

I laughed. "I'll tell her you said that."

"Don't you dare." He threw me a playful glare and then chuckled. We started across the street, but he stopped me with a hand on my arm. "What about your leg?"

Rolling my eyes, I kept going and eased myself off the curb. "If I can get from your truck to the barn without crying 'uncle,' I can make it across the road."

"Fair enough."

My body was sore from moving around off and on at work all day, so getting from one side of the street to the other sucked ass. I refused to let it show, though. Ryan stayed beside me, glancing back and forth occasionally to make sure there weren't any cars coming, and the arm closest to me seemed tense, as if he was poised to catch me if I stumbled. Like hell was I going to stumble. I had this, damn it.

I made it to the other side, and Ryan opened the door for me.

As I headed inside, Ryan glanced back the way we'd come. "You know, I'd really hate to see someone who's afraid of needles wander down this street. Between the acupuncture and the tattoos, there's—"

"Pfft. Half of Mike's patients and probably just as many of Seth's clients say they're afraid of needles."

"How the hell does that work?"

"Different kind of needles," Seth broke in, glancing up from working on a blonde girl's back. "Hey, Nathan. I'm finishing up here. I'll be with you guys in a second."

"Take your time."

While Seth continued tattooing his client, Ryan and I checked out the designs on the wall. They had the kind of shit every tattoo shop had, like banners and hearts, but they were known for their amazing custom designs. Seth could draw incredibly realistic portraits, and Lane had won some national awards for his work. I'd been hesitant to get a tattoo before, but the more time I spent drooling over their work, the more I was seriously considering one.

"So what are you thinking of getting?" I asked.

"Don't know yet." Ryan hooked his thumbs in the pockets of his jeans. "I figure as with everything"—he glanced at me, grinning a little—"I'll know it when I see it."

I swallowed. "So no idea at all?"

Ryan shrugged and shifted his attention back to the artwork. "I kind of know what I want it to mean, just not what it'll be."

"So, what do you want it to mean?"

"Something about being free and out on the road. Not tied down anywhere." Laughing softly, he shook his head. "I don't know. Sounds kind of stupid when I explain it."

"No, it doesn't. Seems quite fitting for you. Why not a motorcycle or something like that?"

Ryan's lips quirked, and he shrugged again. "That might work. A bike and the open road or something." Then he turned to me. "You still thinking about getting a tattoo?" He grinned, and damn if he didn't do a quick down-up with his eyes. "You'd look good with some ink."

I raised an eyebrow. "So I need some ink to—"

"That is so not what I said." He laughed. "I mean… well, let's just say I have an appreciation for hot cars, especially hot cars with some custom paint and a little chrome."

I locked eyes with him. His grin turned a bit sheepish, and as some color rushed into his cheeks, he cleared his throat and broke eye contact.

"I mean, uh… obviously it's a personal thing," he said, almost stammering.

I chuckled and scanned the artwork on the walls. "So what kind of tattoo do you think I should get?"

"Uh…." He shifted beside me. "Maybe something horse related?" He pointed at a sheet of horses and horseshoes. "Like… oh, that one." He tapped a wicked cool line drawing of a dressage horse, one with just enough angles and curves to imply the shape and the extended trot, but without any intricate details. "That's a really interesting one."

"Yeah, it is." I leaned in to examine it closer. "Hmm. Might have to consider it. Question is, where should—" I turned my head, and my heart skipped when I realized that inspecting the drawing had pulled us closer to each other.

Ryan swallowed. "Where should you get it?"

"Yeah."

"I, uh…." He faced the drawing again, focusing intently on it. I wondered if his heart was beating as fast as mine. Maybe that would account for the additional pink in his cheeks right now. Or maybe that was my imagination. Wishful thinking. Something.

I heard movement behind us, and we both turned around. Seth was bandaging up his client.

"I think he's almost done," I said.

"Good. Good." Ryan exhaled, and I wondered if he was as thankful as I was for the diversion.

Seth finished with his client and settled up with her. Once she'd gone, he came up to the counter. "Sorry to keep you guys waiting. What's up?"

"Dragging in a potential client." I smiled. "Seth, this is my friend Ryan. Ryan, Seth."

They shook hands over the counter.

"Nice to meet you," Ryan said. "Nathan's been talking about your work. Thought I'd come check it out for myself."

Seth's gaze slid toward me. "You know I don't pay you until after I've inked him, right?"

"As long as you pay me."

Ryan eyed me but then chuckled and shook his head. "Anyway. Yes, I'm interested in getting a tattoo." He waved a hand at the designs on the wall. "And I do like your work."

"Thanks," Seth said. "See anything you like for yourself, or are you thinking of getting something custom?"

"Probably custom. Biggest question, though, is about where to put it." Ryan gestured over his shoulder. "I've already got one that I'd like to... I don't know, redo. Can you do it?"

"I can cover up a tattoo. Mostly depends on how big and dark the original is and how big and dark the new one will be." Seth motioned for Ryan to turn around. "Can I see the old one?"

"Yeah, sure." In a single movement that I was totally not prepared for, Ryan took off his shirt. He turned around, showing his back to Seth, and I just stood there trying to bring my heart rate back down.

No man had any business being that gorgeous without a shirt. Narrow hips, lean abs, broad shoulders—so hot. *So* fucking hot. He didn't have a six-pack, but his stomach was flat and smooth; probably wouldn't take him long to *get* a six-pack if he were so inclined. Or he could seriously stay just the way he was, because holy fuck.

As Seth inspected the tattoo, I imagined him putting his hand on Ryan and then touching the needle to his skin. Would Ryan jump? Gasp? Or close his eyes and stoically endure the pain?

Get a grip, Nathan.

I shook myself and shifted my attention back to whatever Seth was saying.

"—not a bad-looking tattoo, to be honest. Faded a bit, but that's bound to happen."

"Yeah, but I don't think it's what I want anymore." Ryan faced Seth again, and as he slid his arms into his sleeves, he added, "Being a military brat isn't really who I am anymore, you know?"

"Gotcha." Seth folded his arms loosely across his chest and cocked his head. "The new tattoo will need to be at least as big as that one. Let's talk designs."

THE DOOR banged shut behind us, cutting off the buzzing of the other artist's tattoo needle.

"So you think you're going to get one?" I asked.

Ryan shrugged. "Maybe. We'll see what he comes up with. If I like what he emails me, I'll probably schedule something." He smiled, spinning his keys around his finger. "So, should we head to the barn? Tsarina's probably climbing the walls by now."

Laughing, I nodded. "Yeah, let's go before she drives everyone there insane."

"Good idea. And by the way?" He gestured over his shoulder at the shop. "Your friend is seriously hot." He said it under his breath, as if Seth might hear him through the door.

"You don't have to tell me." I winked. "And you should see his boyfriend."

"Oh yeah?"

"*Smoking* hot."

"Birds of a feather, right?"

I laughed. "They're about as different as two guys can get, but yeah, they're both hot as hell."

Ryan unlocked the truck and opened the passenger side door. "Different how?"

"Well." I gingerly hoisted myself onto the seat. "One's a minister and the other is Mr. Skeptic."

Ryan laughed. "And they don't kill each other?"

"So far, so good."

Once I was situated, he closed my door and went around to the driver side. As he started the truck, he said, "It really amazes me how people can make it work when they're that different."

"It amazes me people can make it work at all, to be honest."

He gave a quiet, bitter laugh. "Yeah, really."

"Not a fan of relationships?"

"Nope." He put his hand behind my seat and twisted around so he could back out of the space. As the truck rolled back, he added, "Not a fan of using people or being used, so… no."

"Wow. And I thought I was cynical."

Ryan chuckled. He shifted into Drive and pulled out onto the road. "It probably doesn't help that I grew up on military bases. Seems like half those people are only in it for the benefits and the guaranteed piece of ass."

"So that stuff's true?"

"Oh yeah. There are plenty of couples who work out fine, but most of the ones I knew?" He shook his head. "Believe me, it's enough to put any military brat off marriage."

"I can imagine."

"Also probably doesn't help that my love life never got off to a good start." He paused to make a left turn, and after he'd straightened out, continued. "I dated a guy in high school for a little while. Thought he was amazing until I realized he was more attracted to my car than he was to me."

I wrinkled my nose. "Really? What a dick."

"That's what I said." Ryan rolled his eyes. "And then I saw Army wives 'upgrading' to Air Force husbands, enlisted spouses ditching their partners for officers...." Sighing, he shook his head. "Just really left a bad taste in my mouth, you know?"

"God, yes. I think I'm a slower learner, though."

"How do you figure?"

"I saw all that crap from the time I was a kid, especially once I started dating in high school. But you know how teenagers are. Everything bad happens to everyone *else*. They picked the wrong guy, or they were stupid to let someone walk all over them. Whatever. It wasn't going to happen to me." I shook my head. "After my last two boyfriends? Believe me, I figured out I wasn't any more immune to that bullshit than anyone else."

"Yeah?" Ryan glanced at me, tapping his fingers on the wheel. "Bad breakups?"

"No, no. The breakups were wonderful. It was the relationships that sucked."

He laughed. "That bad, huh?"

"That bad." I picked at the fraying edge of the cast on my hand. "One was constantly negative and nasty, and the other had a little difficulty with the word 'monogamy.'"

"Ouch."

"Seriously." I rested my elbow beneath the window. "Which is why I am *over* relationships."

"Amen to that."

CHAPTER TEN

I'D TAUGHT a few people to ride over the years, and Ryan was definitely the fastest learner. Maybe it was his experience as a kid that made everything else come naturally. He'd even caught on to posting in a single lesson—and God, the way his thighs flexed through his jeans as he rose and sat in time with the horse's gait made my head spin.

It was just as well he had a clue what he was doing. The lessons I'd promised were turning out to be half-assed at best. I'd genuinely set out to give him proper instructions, and each day I told myself I would do exactly that, but what could I say? It was hard to concentrate when he was in the saddle. I was supposed to be shouting "Heels *down*!" and "Shoulders *back*!" and all those things trainers barked at their students, but I kept catching myself staring at his shoulders and not giving a damn if they were back or slouched. God help me if the summer got any hotter and he started taking off his shirt while he rode.

Before my pulse went haywire again, I called out, "That's enough for today." *Is it ever.* "Let's put her away so she can rest a bit before she eats." *And so I can catch my breath.*

He eased her down from a trot to a walk. When we'd first started, he'd bounced awkwardly during transitions like that, but he was so much better now. Just a few lessons, and he could already sit easily while she downshifted. Once she was walking, he loosened his reins, and as she stretched her neck, he leaned down to pat her shoulder. His hips twisted slightly, and Tsarina obediently turned and started toward me.

He brought her to a gentle halt beside the bleachers. She lowered her head over the rail, nuzzling my hand and no doubt searching for yet another treat.

"I'm impressed." I stroked her face as Ryan dismounted. "You really are a natural."

He landed beside her, tiny clouds of dust jumping up beside his boots. "Thanks." He carefully pulled the reins over her head. "By the way, I figured out why she keeps spooking over there." He nodded toward the southeast corner of the arena.

"Oh yeah?"

"There's a bird's nest behind the post. You can barely see it, but I think she can hear it."

I sighed heavily and eyed Tsarina. "A bird's nest? Really?"

Ryan laughed. "She's going to be thrilled when the chicks start trying to leave the nest."

"You big baby." I patted her neck. "They're only birds."

Tsarina just snorted.

"So." Ryan grinned. "Should we do this again tomorrow?"

"Oh, yes." I gulped. "Yes. Definitely."

Ryan winked. "Looking forward to it."

So am I, my friend. So am I.

AFTER ANOTHER incredibly fun climb up the six flights of stairs to my apartment, Ryan and I stopped outside my door.

"Thanks for helping me up again," I said.

"Anytime. And, as always, if you need anything else, let me know. Even if it's just to get out of the house once in a while so you don't get stir-crazy."

"Thanks." I smiled, and he returned it.

"Well, um." He cleared his throat. "I guess I should get going. Another early morning."

"Yeah, I have to get up too." Our eyes met. Lingered. My heart sped up.

"Anyway." He broke eye contact and took a step back, inching toward the stairs. "Have a good night."

"Yeah, you too." I started toward the door but hesitated. "Oh. By the way, just so we're clear, you're not obligated to do any of the rest of this stuff. Just keeping Tsarina exercised is way more than I could ask for."

A smile I couldn't quite decipher—sort of shy, but sort of not—spread across his lips. "You really think I'm doing any of this out of obligation?"

"I...." *I don't know.* "Why *are* you doing it?"

The smile remained. So did the eye contact. With a subtle shrug, he said, "Why wouldn't I?"

"Well, I coldcocked you across the face the day we met, for one thing."

Ryan laughed, dropping his gaze. "And my face broke your hand, so we're square."

Our eyes met again.

I cleared my throat. "Then… why…."

He stepped a little closer, chasing away all the oxygen in the hallway. "Isn't it obvious?"

"Um…." I tried not to choke on my own breath. "You might have to break it down for me. Tell me like I'm stupid."

He laughed again, quietly, and I felt it this time, warm and soft across my lips, because he was moving in closer. And before I could fit all that together in my head, he pressed his lips to mine.

I couldn't move. If not for the crutch and the cast, I had no idea if or how I'd have stayed upright.

Was this happening?

Ryan tilted his head a little, his soft goatee brushing my chin, and I finally remembered how to move enough to part my lips. We both sighed as the kiss deepened slightly. His hand moved to the side of my neck, and he held on gently, as if he'd needed to steady himself a little. He kissed me like he was nervous and confident all at once—scared to death to make the move, but determined all the same to do it.

The response below my belt wasn't remotely chaste, but the kiss itself was. This was so… different. A subtle kiss, lips only and no tongue at all, without pressing our bodies together, and it brought my thoughts to a standstill no differently than if he'd slammed me up against the wall and kissed me like we were going to fuck right then and there.

A first kiss was usually a one-way ticket to a one-night stand or an awkward exit, but this one…. I didn't know where anything was going now. Leaning half on a crutch and half on him, lips moving so slowly with his, I was sure the world had stopped, and if and when it started again hinged on when this kiss reached its eventual end.

I was the first to pull away, and when I met his eyes, the world still wasn't moving underneath us. His eyebrows were up, pulled together in an unspoken question, his expression full of nerves and doubts and even a little fear. No, more than a little fear. Like he was a breath away from "I'm sorry" or "God, I don't know what came over me."

Sure enough, after a moment of stunned silence, he drew back a little more and found some air: "I'm sorry, that—"

"Don't apologize," I whispered. "And please don't tell me it won't happen again."

He held my gaze. "Really?"

I smiled. "Do you think I didn't like you kissing me?"

"Well, no. But I... um, I guess I hadn't...." He swallowed. "I hadn't thought beyond this point, to be honest. Figured I'd...." He broke eye contact, cheeks coloring again. Goddamn him, he even made shy sexy.

"Figured you'd kiss me and go from there?"

He laughed almost tonelessly. "Something like that."

"It's worked so far. Why don't you kiss me again and go from there?"

His head snapped up and our eyes met again. His were wide with surprise.

I grinned in spite of these unfamiliar nerves fluttering in the pit of my stomach. "I don't bite."

Ryan laughed again, and again it was nearly silent, and I was so close to begging him to take me up on the offer and please, please, please kiss me again, but then he touched my neck and leaned in and did exactly that.

His lips were more confident this time but still tentative. I took the reins from him, putting a hand behind his neck and holding him firmly as I teased his lips apart with my tongue. Ryan shivered, pulling in a breath through his nose as I slipped the tip of my tongue under his. His fingers drifted up into my hair, sending goose bumps down the back of my neck.

I pulled back, pausing to sweep my tongue across my lips. "Do you… um…." I swallowed. This was the moment when I'd usually either feign tiredness and call it a night, or invite him in to check out my bedroom ceiling, but neither option seemed like a natural progression with Ryan. "Do you want to come in for a while?"

"Sure. You probably shouldn't stay on that leg too long anyway." His teeth snapped shut and his eyes widened. "I… that's not what I meant. I—"

"It's okay." I laughed as I dug my house key out of my pocket. "I do need to put it up." I paused, key halfway to the door. "We can just, um, hang out in the living room for a while?"

Ryan nodded. "That works."

He seemed relieved by the idea. Weird. He'd been the one to make the move, but the assurance we weren't headed straight for my bedroom calmed him.

I keyed us into the apartment, and we went into the living room. Brad was probably already asleep, so we moved quietly and only turned on the small lamp beside the couch, which lit up the room with a soft, dim glow.

Ever since I'd broken my leg, the simple act of relaxing on my goddamned couch had become more complicated than drunken calculus. Getting from a vertical position to a horizontal one. Pillows against my back if I wanted to sit up. Mountains of pillows and blanket under the cast whether I wanted to sit up or lie down. Arranging the mountains and the piles so the slightest movement wouldn't cause a bedding avalanche and let everyone else in the apartment complex hear my extensive repertoire of profanity.

Doing it on my own was a royal pain in the ass, especially since I had zero manual dexterity with my right hand. *That's what you get for slugging someone, idiot.* At least I had help this time, and I had to admit, the ridiculous task was a blessing in disguise. It gave us something to do, something to focus on and keep our hands busy in the wake of that moment in the hallway.

Finally I was situated, and no adjustments remained to keep us distracted. I was sitting upright on the couch, my leg stretched across the cushions and propped up against the back, and Ryan had pulled an ottoman up next to me. Sitting on that, he was just inches away, close enough to touch, nothing but my plaster-encased hand and a few inches of cushion between us.

And once again, our eyes met.

I was usually so confident with things like this. I made the first move. I was the first to go in for the kiss, the first to tug at a zipper. But this was different somehow, in a way I couldn't begin to define.

Holding my gaze, Ryan closed some of the distance. My heart sped up. It was almost like I'd somehow convinced myself I'd imagined that moment in the hallway, and now it was becoming real again. Every nerve ending in my body lit up like a glowing ember coming back to life, but then Ryan stopped. A ragged breath rushed past my lips. He pulled back a little. Whatever confidence had driven him before was suddenly absent.

I curved my hand around the back of his neck and lifted my head off the pillow, and we came together somewhere in the middle.

The kiss was deeper this time, more exploratory now that the *holy shit, you kissed me* had worn off. He didn't just open to me, he gave as good as he got, sliding his tongue past mine.

Our hands were almost completely still. Mine rested on the side of his neck. His cradled the back of my head, occasionally stroking or gently grasping my hair.

I was hardly a virgin, but this was like nothing I'd ever experienced. Making out was usually foreplay. An appetizer before the groping and sucking and fucking, or something to tide us over until we *could* grope and suck and fuck. This wasn't. This time it was an act in and of itself. Somehow deep down I knew we wouldn't be sleeping together tonight, that no clothes were coming off and any orgasm I had would be after he'd gone. There would be this much and no more with him, and there wasn't an ounce of frustration in that knowledge. Nothing but complete surrender to his kiss, to his fingers in my hair, to the sweetly erotic way we just tasted each other without demanding anything further. There was no craving for release, because that was exactly what this was: the slow, resonating release of the tension I hadn't even realized had been growing between us since the beginning.

I had no idea how much time passed before we finally came up for air. We were both breathing hard, both holding on to each other a little tighter, and my God, I was hard, but I didn't want this to go any further tonight. It was too good like this. Pushing it would only ruin it, I was sure.

Our foreheads touched.

"Damn, it's late." Ryan sighed. "I have to work tomorrow."

"Me too."

He kissed me again, lightly this time. "I should go."

"Maybe we could see each other tomorrow?" I ran my fingers through his short hair. "After work?"

Ryan smiled. "I can pick you up at the clinic."

Returning the smile, I said, "I'm off at five."

He sat up a little, stretching his back, which must have been aching after leaning toward me for so long. "Before I go, do you need a hand getting from here into—" He stopped abruptly. "Um…."

"The bedroom?" I asked.

"Yeah." His smile was so adorably shy. "I meant because of your leg. Not, um…."

"I could use the help, actually." I chewed my lip. "With getting off the couch. I can handle it from there. You don't mind?"

He shook his head. "Not at all."

We carefully shuffled pillows and cushions around so I could move, and he helped me to my feet.

And suddenly we were against each other again, and his arm was around my waist and our mouths were only a few inches apart. His kiss hadn't cooled on my lips yet, and though I wasn't hard anymore, it wouldn't take much to get me back to full attention again. He was here, against me, and my whole body wanted to respond to that look in his eyes.

Stay with me tonight, I wanted to say. But how to tell him I didn't want to have sex? I just wanted to stay exactly like we'd been in the hallway and on the couch, holding on and kissing and occasionally staring at each other in utter bewilderment. Maybe eventually we'd get to the stripping down and the flesh and the friction, but all I wanted right now was for him to kiss me like that again. For the rest of the night. Or even just once before he left.

I didn't dare shift my center of gravity too far, but all I had to do was lift my chin and he got the message. He kissed me again, slowly wrapping his arms around me and pulling our bodies together. His erection pressed against mine, and though I didn't want to spoil this by going too far, I swore if I could have bent both my knees, I would've been on the floor sucking his cock right then.

His lips left mine, but neither of us pulled back, and a second later I kissed him again. That one lingered too, long past anything like a good-night kiss.

Finally he broke the kiss and whispered, "I should go."

Please don't.

"Okay," I said. "See you tomorrow at five?"

Ryan's smile made my pulse go haywire. "Absolutely."

We moved to the door, exchanged one more kiss—just a light one this time—and then he was gone. After I'd closed the door behind him, I rested my forehead against it as I turned the dead bolt.

He took two steps and stopped. Hesitating? Checking his phone or something? Glancing over his shoulder and thinking about backtracking?

I'm here. Right here. All you have to do is turn around and come back.

I held my breath. Listened. Begged my heart to slow down so I could hear him over it. Wondered what the hell we'd do if he did come back.

But then his footsteps faded down the hall and finally down the stairs.

I turned around and leaned against the door. Staring up at the ceiling, I couldn't make sense of anything that had happened from the moment we'd reached the top of the steps until now. If not for the tingling on my lips and the rather uncomfortable hard-on, I'd have been convinced I'd imagined the entire thing.

I closed my eyes and exhaled. Considering how we'd met, I should have learned by this point to expect the unexpected when it came to Ryan.

He'd been helping me out, and he'd been flirting in his own subtle way, and then suddenly he was kissing me, and it made perfect sense for us to be kissing like that. Except it didn't. But it did. I'd been tripping over my own feet around him since day one, and I couldn't put my finger on anything I *dis*liked about him, so why the hell not? Well, besides the fact that I hadn't expected him to be the one to make the move.

And then there was the fact that a kiss like that meant sex was a possibility, and sex sometimes led to relationships, and relationships led to shit I had no desire to deal with again, but....

Christ.

So he'd made the move I hadn't had the balls to make, and now we'd crossed this line, and... now what? I didn't have a clue. When I'd punched him on the trail, I probably hadn't knocked him half as senseless as his gentle kiss had just knocked me.

I adjusted my grip on my crutch. Then I headed down the hall to my bedroom, though I didn't see sleep in my near future. I was losing my mind. Maybe instead of getting my leg and hand checked at the ER, I should have had the doc check out my goddamned head.

CHAPTER ELEVEN

SOMEHOW I was supposed to concentrate at work.

I'd gotten the hang of maneuvering through the day with these damned casts on and was even starting to write quasilegibly with my left hand. I hadn't, however, banked on having to work with Ryan on my mind like this.

Last night hadn't left me unsatisfied, but it had damn sure left me wanting more. What would it be like to kiss him like that while we were both naked? As if it hadn't been hot enough fully clothed. I wanted to know what he felt and tasted like when he'd reached that point of no return, when he was too turned on to think about anything except climaxing. Climaxing on me, in me, in my mouth, anywhere. Jesus Christ, he probably made the most amazing sounds when he—

The clinic's front door opened, dragging me out of my wandering thoughts as Jason strolled in behind his stepson, Dylan.

"Hey," he said. "I just came by to grab—" He stopped abruptly and did a double take at my leg.

I resisted the urge to groan. "Please tell me Mike's already told you the story."

"Yeah, he did." Jason chuckled. "But he didn't tell me you were practically in a body cast."

"Oh, go f—" I glanced at Dylan, then back at Jason. "Bite me."

He just laughed.

"Whatever, dude," I said. "So what are you doing here?"

"I'm taking Dylan to his dentist appointment, and Michael forgot to leave his insurance card at the house."

"Oh. Okay. I'll go let him know you're here." I started to get up.

"No, no." Jason gestured for me to sit back down. "We're going to be early for his appointment as it is. No sense jarring you to save me two minutes."

"I can get around." I pushed myself up. "I'm stuck this way for another two months, so I'd better be able to move a little bit without help."

"Don't worry about it," he insisted. "Michael's probably with a patient anyway, isn't he?"

I glanced down the hall. Mike actually had three patients back there right now, and I didn't know which one he was with at the moment, so I sat back down. "You win this one, Davis."

Jason laughed. "Don't I always?"

"Ass," I said just low enough so Dylan wouldn't hear me.

One of the doors opened at the end of the hall. Jason glanced that way, but no expression registered on his face. Then one of Mike's longtime patients stepped into view and stopped in front of my desk to pay for her appointment.

After she'd settled up and scheduled her next visit, I said, "We'll see you on Friday. Have a good day, Mrs. Carson."

"You too, sweetie." She smiled. "I hope your leg gets better quickly."

"Thanks."

As she headed out, more movement at the end of the hall drew Jason's attention, and this time his whole face lit up. I couldn't see Mike, but I was pretty sure he had the same expression. Those two had been together for a while now—I'd lost track—and they still reacted like that whenever they saw each other. Certainly a far cry from when they'd started out and Mike had been afraid of anyone—himself included—realizing he was gay.

At least someone had gotten this whole relationship business down. My jaded side worried they'd one day go down the same road as Brad and Jeff, but I hoped not. Like Brad and Jeff, they deserved that elusive happy ending, and I sincerely hoped they'd have it together.

Oblivious to my inner pessimism, Mike gave Jason the insurance card he needed, and then they exchanged a quick kiss and a brief glance before Jason left with Dylan. Mike probably had no idea he still had that goofy grin on his face long after his man had left. All cynicism aside, I swore those two would be that hundred-year-old couple in the nursing home who were still so cuddly that all the other old people kept telling them to get a room.

Mike was by my desk, jotting some notes in a chart, when the familiar beat-up black truck with Oregon plates pulled up in front of the clinic. The glare on the windshield obscured Ryan's face, but my heart quickened even though I couldn't see him. Then the driver's side door opened, and my stomach fluttered as soon as I saw that familiar tattoo sticking out from beneath a white T-shirt sleeve.

"*That's* the guy you're dating?"

"What?" I glanced at Mike. "Okay, first, I didn't say a word, and second, we're not dating. He's riding Tsarina for me. That's it."

Mike's face had *bullshit* written all over it. Mine was probably getting red if the heat in my cheeks was anything to go by.

"Whatever," I said, but I couldn't help smiling.

Mike just shook his head and laughed. As Ryan approached the door, Mike turned around, feigning interest in the chart in his hand and muttering under his breath, "Well done, Nathan. Well done."

I bit back another protest that we weren't actually dating, but an odd feeling twisted in my stomach.

The door opened, and Ryan smiled as he pulled off his sunglasses. "Ready to go?"

"Almost." I glanced at Mike. "You need anything else before I go?"

"Nope. Have a good night." His gaze slid toward Ryan, and then he winked at me. I glared back at him, but at least Ryan didn't seem to notice the exchange. He didn't comment, anyway.

After I'd clocked out and gathered my things, I followed Ryan out and got into the truck. As I buckled my seat belt, that odd feeling in my gut was still there. Especially after last night, there was no telling myself this was about riding lessons and atonement from the accident. Or that whatever we were doing this evening wasn't a date.

He was also leaving in a few months to take a job someplace else. Whatever happened between us wouldn't have a chance to get off the ground before he headed for the horizon. There was safety in that. Reassurance that I couldn't get my heart broken because there wasn't time to get my heart involved.

My body, however, could get involved with this guy until the end of days if he kissed me again like he did last night. Which I hoped he would. Soon.

"Nathan?"

"Hmm?" I blinked, wondering how long I'd been lost in my own thoughts. "Sorry, what?"

He cocked his head. "You okay? You zoned out a bit."

I nodded. "Yeah. Yeah, I'm fine. But I was thinking, um, do you want to skip the lesson tonight?"

He swallowed, looking equal parts intrigued and unnerved. "What else did you have in mind?"

I held his gaze, hoping he'd make the connection and not make me say it out loud. "You tell me."

"I asked you first." He leaned across the console. "Skipping the lesson was *your* idea." But before I could speak, Ryan kissed me, and even the cast couldn't stop my knees from shaking.

Against his lips, I said, "I was thinking something along these lines."

"Hmm, me too." His kiss was lighter this time. "Do you want to go back to my place?"

My heart sped up. "Do you?"

"I do. And I think you might like it." He leaned in and whispered in my ear, "It's on the ground floor."

A nervous but genuine laugh burst out of me. "Ooh, tell me more."

"Hmm." He paused to kiss beneath my ear until I shivered. "How about I show you instead?"

"Please do."

MAKING OUT hadn't been foreplay last night, but it definitely was now.

We'd barely said a word on the way to his apartment, and I hadn't bothered to take in the scenery in his living room or the short hallway leading to his bedroom. There was one place we both wanted to be, and that place was here, on his bed, lost in a deep, breathless kiss.

We weren't just kissing for the sake of kissing tonight. This was hotter, hungrier, complementing the way we held on to each other and tried to get closer and closer to each other. His body was perfect on top of mine. If there hadn't been this damned cast on my leg, we probably would have fit together like we were made for this, his hips settling between my legs and my hands sliding down the muscles and grooves of his back.

Everything about Ryan, from the way he touched me to the way he kissed me, was both tentative and assertive. He was timid—hesitating every time he tried something new as if to make sure I wouldn't protest—but he was aggressive at the same time, not only kissing and touching but *claiming*.

I could be as toppy as the next guy, but with Ryan, I surrendered. I loved his subtle aggression, the way he took what he wanted, but everything he did still had an undercurrent of *is this okay?*

Ryan shifted his weight onto one arm. My skin tingled as his other hand disappeared between us, and when his hand slid over the front of my shorts, I gasped, pressing against his palm. I mirrored him, cupping him through his jeans. Oh, Lord, he'd been blessed. Just the right size.

Please tell me you have condoms and lube, Ryan. We're going to need them.

I licked my lips. "Maybe now's a good time to ask if you're a top or a bottom."

He tensed a little. "No preference. You?"

"Either." I kissed him lightly. "I do prefer the bottom, though." *Especially if you're as big as you feel through your clothes.*

Ryan relaxed. Sort of. "I guess that makes me a top tonight, doesn't it?"

"I guess it does. But don't expect me to be a passive bottom."

He grinned. "I wouldn't want you to be."

"Good." I steadied him with a hand on his shoulder and raised my head off the pillow to kiss his neck. His masculine scent gave me goose bumps, and the warmth of his skin against my lips was beyond arousing. Ryan tilted his head back, then to the side, alternately exposing more hot flesh to my lips and rubbing against me like a cat.

"Fuck, that's amazing," he breathed, the wonder and pure arousal in his voice making me shiver. The more I explored his throat, the more his hips ground against mine, the underside of his erection rubbing back and forth through our clothes. I nipped the side of his neck, and his shudder resonated right through me.

"Fuck," he whispered again, and nudged me away from his neck and searched for my mouth. He kissed me and ground his hips harder against mine.

As I was struggling to find the words to tell him we should get some of these clothes off, he broke the kiss and sat up over me, and as I held my breath and watched, he pulled off his shirt.

Jesus fuck, he was fit. He wasn't one of those gym rats whose tendons and muscle fibers were visible from space, but his biceps and his forearms were noticeably defined, especially where the tattoo's lines and curves emphasized the contour of his muscle. His abs were smooth, flat, and just begging to be touched.

I ran my hand up the center of his abs, up to the thin fan of dark hair on this chest. "It should be illegal for you to wear a shirt. Just so you know."

He laughed softly, his cheeks coloring. How a man that gorgeous could be that shy, I had no idea, but he wore the shyness as well as he wore ink and those faded jeans that needed to come off *right now*.

Obviously we were on a similar wavelength, because as he came down to kiss me again, he started unzipping my shorts.

The casts eliminated any possibility of removing my shorts and boxers—or any of my clothing, for that matter—in a graceful or remotely sexy manner, but Ryan didn't seem to mind. Between us, we stripped off the rest of his clothes and mine, and my God, he was as gorgeous below the now-absent belt as he was above it. Powerful legs, narrow hips, and a very hard cock that was exactly the way I liked it: long, thick, without reaching terrifying porn-star proportions.

With nothing else between us, he lowered himself on top of me, and we both shuddered when his cock pressed against mine again. He came down all the way, his body sinking onto mine, abs and chest meeting one warm inch at a time, and I wrapped my arms around him, not giving a damn about the awkward weight of the plaster on my right one.

"Arms getting tired yet?" I asked.

"Nope. I could do this all night."

"Good."

He kissed me lightly, then started down my neck. My mouth formed toneless curses as he inched down the side of my throat and past my collarbone. His lips were soft against my chest. He made his way to my nipple, and his eyes flicked up to meet mine as he gently bit it. I moaned and let my head fall back onto the pillow, arching my spine off the bed to press my body against his, and he slid his hands under my back. He headed lower, taking his sweet time and teasing my abs with his light kisses. I could almost imagine that sensual, talented mouth on my dick, and I was already desperate to return the favor before he'd even gone down on me.

He continued toward my hip, and then farther, and I nearly levitated off the bed as his lips slid over my cock. I dug my teeth into my lower lip and gripped his hair. His lips and tongue were going to drive me insane, I just knew it, and if I could have moved at all, I'd have thrust upward, fucked into that amazing mouth.

I wanted him. Holy fuck, I wanted him. I wanted to know how much power he had in that gorgeous, toned body, and I wanted him fucking me until we both came.

But right alongside that desire was something else. Something I'd never felt in a moment like this. It was like an inkling of panic that hadn't quite broken open yet. That sense that nothing had happened yet, but it *would*, I was sure of it. I had no reason to distrust Ryan, and I wouldn't have been in his bedroom if I did. Still, a vision flickered through my mind of being pinned down, immobile, unable to fight back effectively. Of being fucked at someone else's whim. What if he was too rough and he hurt me? What if I wanted to stop?

Then the panic broke: I couldn't move. Not fast and not far, no matter how much I wanted to or how badly I needed to get away.

Ryan raised his head. "Something wrong?"

He'd caught on, so he was in tune with me. To my responses. I could trust him, right? What was I so worried about? This was ridiculous. He'd back off at the first sign of distress, like he was doing right now.

But my heart wouldn't slow down.

"What?" Ryan moved up closer to me and touched my face, furrowing his brow. "You okay?"

I took a few deep breaths, willing my heart rate to come back down. This was stupid. What was the matter with me? I tried to shift, as if I could subtly shake away some of this nervous energy, but the thick block of heavy weight encasing my leg wouldn't let me, and it reminded me why I'd been so wound up to begin with.

Ryan moved to the side, lying next to me so he was no longer on top. "Nathan?"

"Listen, I'm…." I bit my lip, embarrassment and frustration vying for dominance. I sighed and ran a hand through my hair, my heart sinking as the mood quickly died.

"What's wrong?" His hand came to rest on my shoulder, a reassuring touch from the same hand that had been teasing me a moment ago.

I couldn't quite meet his eyes. "It's stupid."

He squeezed my arm gently. "Try me."

"I'm kind of a… control freak, I guess. Only time I ever tried handcuffs or anything like that, I freaked out, and it wasn't because I didn't trust the guy I was with. I just didn't like being confined. I need to know, at any given moment, that I can take myself out of a situation." I tapped the edge of a fingernail on my cast.

"And with this thing? I can barely get out of a chair without help. In a way, it's like a handcuff I can't take off." I sighed. "And it makes me feel like I couldn't put a stop to things if I wanted to."

Ryan took my hand. "We don't have to go any further if you aren't comfortable."

I exhaled, equal parts embarrassed and relieved. "I'm sorry."

"Don't be." He reached down and pulled the sheet up over us. Its coolness underscored the warmth of his body still pressed against mine. Both relief and guilt crept in. He wasn't pushing and he hadn't gotten upset, which made me feel even guiltier for putting a stop to things.

I turned toward him and combed my fingers through his hair. "For the record, it's not that I don't trust you. I wouldn't have gone this far with you if I didn't. I—"

"I understand," he said softly. "You're with someone new, and you've got that thing"—he nodded toward my cast—"keeping you from moving. You don't have to justify yourself."

"But I do want us to…." I swallowed, wondering when I'd turned into a schoolkid who couldn't say the words. "Just not tonight."

"Relax." He touched my face, and his long, gentle kiss was so sweet it almost brought tears to my eyes. "You won't have the cast on forever, and I'm not in any hurry."

"A few—" I blinked, drawing back so I could see him. "You're willing to wait? Until the cast comes off?"

"Of course. Why wouldn't I?"

"I don't…." *Because no other man I've ever dated would have been.* "I don't know."

"I want you to enjoy this too," he said. "If you're not comfortable, then…."

"Thank you," I whispered, and kissed him.

I didn't expect the kiss to last, but it did. Ryan was tentative again, not timid now so much as cautious, but as I held him tighter, he did the same to me, and his hardening cock brushed my hip.

He quickly drew back. "Sorry, I'm—"

"Don't be. I still… I want you to come."

"I thought you wanted to stop," he said as he leaned in to kiss me again. "If you don't want—*oh*, fuck." His whole body tensed as I closed my hand around his cock. I stroked him slowly until he was fully hard again.

"Even if we aren't going to fuck tonight," I whispered, "I still want you to come."

He groaned softly. His hand rested on my stomach. "I want to make you come too. But only… I don't want to push you if…."

I gently grasped his wrist and guided his hand down to my own erection, then returned my hand to his. He didn't hesitate. His fingers closed around me, and we stroked each other at the same frantic speed. We panted against each other's lips, thrust into each other's hands, tried to kiss and hold on to each other but couldn't find a rhythm that wasn't *faster, faster, please don't stop, faster*….

"Get on top," I said.

He hesitated. "You won't be able to move."

I tapped a knuckle on my cast. "I can't move anyway." I kissed him again. "I trust you. Get on top."

"But you… you said it bothers you." He ran his fingers down the side of my face. "If you can't move."

"Will you stop if I ask you to?"

Drawing back a little, he nodded. "Of course."

"Then I'll be okay. As long as I know you'll stop...."

He chewed his lip. "I just don't want to freak you out."

"You won't."

He still didn't move. Then he inched closer, draping his arm over me. "The second you're even a little uncomfortable, you'll say so?"

"Absolutely."

Another moment of hesitation, but then he moved over me, and I nudged his hand away so I could wrap my fingers around both our cocks.

"Oh fuck," he groaned as I started stroking us both.

"Like that?"

He just whimpered softly and came down to kiss me. I stroked faster. His hips started moving, and we both moaned as he thrust into my fist and against my cock, the friction intense to the point of almost painful, and white light crept into my peripheral vision.

"Oh God," he breathed. "Oh…. God…." His forehead touched mine, his skin hot and damp, and he was shaking now, tense, thrusting erratically and panting. I'd never seen anything more arousing than Ryan falling apart, and when his orgasm crashed through him, drawing a helpless cry from his lips as his slick semen coated my hand and my own cock, I came too, shaking beneath him and stroking us both until I couldn't handle another second.

We both shuddered once more and were still. He didn't lift off me. I didn't let go. Our lips brushed in between rapid, uneven breaths, but we couldn't quite kiss, couldn't quite remember how.

Eventually Ryan got up. He brought me a towel, and we cleaned ourselves up. Neither of us said anything. There wasn't much that could be said right then without ruining this lovely postorgasmic lethargy, and instead of talking, we wrapped up in each other underneath the thin sheet.

Before long, Ryan had dozed off.

Lying beside him, listening to him sleep, I didn't regret the fact that we hadn't gone any further tonight. I'd have been too scared, too nervous, if I'd forced aside my fears and let him fuck me. Now, though, just knowing he was willing to back off and wait *months* to try again had settled something in me. He was forceful when the moment called for it but not when I wanted to stop. Not even a little bit.

I stroked his hair and closed my eyes.

We would. Not tonight. Maybe not tomorrow night.

But we would.

CHAPTER TWELVE

THE NEXT night Brad was out for the evening, and he probably wouldn't be back until late. Assuming, of course, that things with Jeff didn't end in disaster. I had my fingers crossed for their benefit—they both deserved to be happy, with or without each other—but there was a little selfishness involved this time too. I needed the apartment to myself, if only for this *one* night.

As always, Ryan was right on time. I'd left the door unlocked for him, so he let himself in as I carefully got up off the couch.

"Ready to go?" he asked.

"Actually," I said with a nervous grin, "I was thinking we could stay in."

"Oh." He regarded me uncertainly for a moment. "What did you have in mind?"

"I was hoping we could, uh, we could pick up where we left off last night." Just saying the words ramped up my heartbeat, both from nerves and excitement.

He held my gaze. "But I thought…."

"I know." I clumsily narrowed some of the distance between us. "I've been thinking about last night all damned day, though. And I… I want to."

He held my gaze. "You were pretty freaked out last night. I don't want to put you through that again."

"You won't. I'm, uh, I'm not big on being confined. I should've known that might happen and not been quite so blindsided when it did. But now that I've had a chance to work through it in my head, I think I'm okay."

He tilted his head slightly. "You *think* you're okay?"

I nodded. "And just like last night, if I'm not okay, we can stop, right?"

"Of course," he said without a second's hesitation.

I smiled. "That's all I need to know." I came closer. "Stay with me."

Ryan gulped. "You're sure?"

"Are you?"

"If… if you are, yeah. Of course." He put his hands on my waist. "I was serious when I said we could wait until your casts came off."

"I know." I pulled him a little closer. "That's why I don't *want* to wait." I kissed him, and after a second's hesitation, he returned my kiss and wrapped his arms around me.

"I have condoms," I said. "And lube. And I want to use them tonight. With you."

"But you're—"

"I trust you. After last night, I feel safe with you."

"You *are* safe with me, Nathan." He cradled my face in both hands and kissed me gently. "Say the word if you want to stop."

"I will."

"This could get...." He paused and nodded toward my cast. "How exactly do we do this?"

I laughed. "Fortunately, I've already thought about the logistics."

"Have you?"

"I have." I kissed him again. "We'll sort all that out when we get to that point."

"Works for me," he murmured. "I just want...." He looked me up and down, and when our eyes met, he didn't have to finish the sentence. I pulled him to me again, and he closed the rest of the distance. This kind of kiss existed midway between where we'd gone last night and where I hoped we'd go tonight: still tentative, but leaving no room for doubt that we both wanted each other and that we didn't want to stop.

"Bedroom," I said.

He nodded wordlessly.

It took a little extra effort to get me into the bedroom and out of my clothes, but I didn't care and Ryan didn't seem to mind.

We'd barely thrown off the last stitch of clothing before I was back in his arms. Ryan could be shy, and he could be aggressive, and right now he was the latter. He slid his hand over my cock, pressing just right to create the most mind-blowing friction. I felt around blindly, my sense of direction all kinds of fucked-up because of his touch, and finally wrapped my fingers around his dick. We made out and stroked each other, and his hips thrust against my hand in a pantomime of how I hoped they'd move when he fucked me.

His fingers tightened around me as he broke the kiss with a whispered "Jesus Christ...."

"Like that?"

"Mm-hmm." He stroked a little faster. "You?"

"Oh. God. Yes."

His lips curved into a grin against mine, and then he kissed me again, full-on and deep and breathless, and if I could've moved at all, I'd have fucked his hand the way he fucked mine, and I probably would have come, because holy hell….

I shivered and pulled away enough to murmur, "Fuck me." Another kiss. "Now. I don't want to wait."

"N-now?" His eyes widened. "You don't—"

"Please." I didn't care that I was begging. I never begged. Ever. But goddamn, I wanted him.

Ryan licked his lips. His body tensed, and when he met my eyes, his were full of nervousness. "Do you, um…." He gulped. "Condoms?"

I nodded and gestured at the drawer beside the bed.

He reached over and pulled out the condoms and lube. "And how exactly are we going to do this so we don't hurt your leg?"

"Like this." I turned onto my side.

"Are you sure?" He ran a hand down my arm. "With your cast leg on top?"

I nodded and reached back to trail my fingers down his thigh. "Otherwise I can't touch you."

"Is it comfortable?"

"It's fine." Okay, so it wasn't great, but damn if I was going to lie on top of my good arm and not be able to touch him, so I'd make do. We both put a pillow between my cast and my other leg. Once I was situated, Ryan settled in behind me. Jesus, the heat of his body took my breath away, and his hard cock pressed against my ass was almost more than I could take. Last night I'd been afraid of not being able to stop things if I'd wanted to. Now I was sure I'd lose my mind if he didn't fuck me *right now*.

He leaned away for a second, and when he came back, he slipped his hand between my legs. Cool, lubed fingers pressed against my ass, blurring my vision as they pushed in.

"Fuck," I breathed.

He nuzzled my neck. "This comfortable?"

I'm supposed to answer while you're finger-fucking me? "Mm-hmm." I bit my lip. His goatee tickled my skin, and his lips and breath were soft enough to send a delicious tingle down my spine. *Fuck me, Ryan. Please....*

"I want you so bad," he breathed. "But are you sure about this?"

"Very."

"Do—"

"Fuck me," I growled. "Hurry up."

He laughed softly and pressed another kiss below my ear. "Give me a second." Then he slid his fingers free. His body was suddenly no longer touching mine, and I wanted to reach back and find him and drag him to me again, but the sound of foil tearing calmed me down.

Behind me, something rustled. Ryan cursed under his breath. More rustling. His hands must have been shaking. I wondered if he was as turned on as I was, or if he was nervous, or what, but then he was against me again, and all I wanted was to feel him.

He guided his cock to me. This was it. We were doing this.

A cold prickle worked its way up my spine. All the fear I'd pushed aside earlier came back. My whole body tensed. Couldn't move.

"You okay?" he asked.

I took and released a deep breath, willing myself to relax. I was safe. I knew I was. If I wanted to stop, Ryan would. I didn't have the faintest doubt that he'd stop again at the first sign of trouble. But the weight of the plaster was still there, reminding me of my immobility.

Ryan started to draw away. "Nathan?"

"I'm good." I reached back and grabbed his leg. "Please. I want this."

"Me too. But… I don't…."

"I'm okay." I kneaded his leg and pressed back against him as much as I could. "Ryan. Please."

He hesitated but then relaxed. "Remember, all you have to do is say the word if you want to stop."

I nodded.

The slick presence of his cock made my breath catch. Not nerves now—not much—just anticipation. Pure need. And a few nerves. I could do this. I wanted this.

Ryan kissed beneath my ear. "If it helps, I'm nervous too." He exhaled hard as he guided his cock into place. "Never done this before."

I had to admit, his nerves settled mine a bit. "Never tried this position? You've been missing out."

"It's not that." He pressed harder against my ass, the slightest bit of pressure away from being inside me. "I've never done this. At all."

I didn't have time to put the pieces together before he applied that slightest bit of pressure, and the head of his cock slid into me, and my vision blurred.

"Oh God," he whispered, his ragged breath warm against my neck. He withdrew a little, then started to push in again.

"You're…." I licked my lips. "Y-you're… a virgin?"

A rush of laughter brushed my ear. "Not anymore."

Disbelief and arousal conspired to keep me silent as he pushed farther inside me. His cock felt so damned good, and it was just the right size, and I leaned back against him to drive him a little deeper. He found a slow, steady rhythm, and then he was all the way in, and his strokes turned to hard thrusts, and—

"F-fuck…." He shuddered. His body tensed against mine, and he forced himself all the way in and stopped. When he shuddered again, his tremors and his release reverberated through me, through my entire body.

I exhaled and slowly relaxed my grasp on the handful of sheets I hadn't realized I'd grabbed. It had been quick, almost too quick, but maybe that wasn't such a bad thing. I hadn't had a chance to panic about my immobility, hadn't had an opportunity to freak out.

"Fuck," he said, panting as he withdrew. "Sorry, I didn't think it would be so fast."

"It's all right." I turned my head and reached back to draw him to me. "Nothing to be sorry for at all."

"But that—"

I cut him off with a light kiss. "It was perfect."

He eyed me skeptically but didn't argue. "I should, um, get rid of this."

I nodded. He got up to take care of the condom and then slid back into bed, facing me, and pulled the sheet up over us.

"You okay?" he asked. "With your leg, I mean?"

I nodded. "Yeah. I'm fine." I ran my fingers down the side of his face. "So this really was your first time?"

His cheeks colored, and he laughed. "You couldn't tell?"

"You sure seemed to know what you were doing."

Ryan laughed again, softer this time. "Didn't seem too complicated. Just didn't… last."

I lifted my head and kissed him lightly. "The next time will."

He smiled and returned my kiss. "I'm looking forward to it."

When he pulled back this time, I asked, "Out of curiosity, how much *have* you done?"

He shrugged. "Oh, I've fooled around a little."

"Ever sucked a cock? Before last night, I mean?"

More color in his cheeks, but to my surprise, he nodded. "Yeah, I have."

I grinned and trailed the backs of my fingers down his arm, over his tattoo. "Some guys think that's where the virginity line is drawn for us. Since not all gay men fuck."

"Either way, this was something new for me."

I stroked his face. "Why didn't you tell me before? I had no idea."

He smiled shyly. "You think it's easy admitting that when you're twenty-five?"

"Okay, maybe not. But if I'd known…."

"You wouldn't have been disappointed?"

"Oh stop. I wasn't disappointed." I broke eye contact. "Honestly, a quick one was probably exactly what I needed this time around."

"Why's that?"

"To make sure…." Though it was a struggle, I made myself find his gaze again. "To make sure I really could handle it." I stroked his face with my fingertips. "I didn't think to ask if this was too much for you, or—"

"It wasn't." He gently clasped my hand and kissed my fingers. "Not at all."

"But you…." I held his gaze. "Why me?"

"Because I wanted you." He kissed me lightly. "I guess I thought, after last night… I mean, what changed *your* mind?"

"The fact that you were willing to wait. It wasn't a game or a test or anything. I... the last thing I expected you to say was that you were perfectly fine waiting until my casts came off, and after you said that, I knew I could trust you."

"I'd never hurt you." His lips quirked, and he trailed a fingertip across the cast on my hand. "Erm, not deliberately, anyway."

I laughed. "I know what you meant."

He chuckled. "Well, I hope it really wasn't a disappointment."

"No, no. Not at all."

He kissed underneath my jaw. "Except you didn't come."

I shivered. "Hmm, no. But you can... oh God...." My back almost levitated off the bed as his lips started downward, inching down my neck and chest one soft, lingering kiss at a time.

I held my breath as he continued over my abs to my painfully hard cock. He didn't have that refined skill of someone who'd given a lot of blow jobs, no signature trick with his hand or his tongue, but his eagerness to please me and turn me on more than made up for that, and there wasn't a thing lacking. God, not a thing. He was the perfect lover, with that single-minded drive to give pleasure like it was some kind of divine offering.

Several times I almost came but made myself hold back because I didn't want this to end. Except I wanted him to get off again too. I wanted him inside me again. I wanted it to last this time so I could feel his breath on my neck and hear him falling apart while I lost my mind. I wanted him to know what it felt like to fuck until every muscle ached and stopping wasn't an option until we'd found release.

"S-stop… stop.…"

He pushed himself up. "Did I do some—"

"Fuck me," I said, breathing hard. "I want you to fuck me again."

Ryan came all the way up and brushed his lips over mine. "I was going to make you come."

"Yes, you were." I shivered beneath him. "But I want… there is nothing in the world like coming while I'm being fucked."

"Well, when you put it like that.…"

We changed position again. Onto my side, a pillow to keep my cast from pressing against my other leg, and after he'd taken a moment to put on another condom, I could barely breathe as he positioned himself behind me.

He guided his cock to me again. Holy fuck, I was so aroused, just that first stroke was enough to make my eyes water. He whimpered softly, pressing his lips to my neck as his hips moved faster.

His lack of experience didn't show as much as he must've thought it did; he moved as easily as this position allowed, sliding in and out with a rhythm that was equal parts slow and desperate.

I closed my eyes, mouthing silent profanity, and finally managed to say, "F-faster."

"Not yet," he whispered. "I want it to last this time." He took a long, deep stroke, giving me as much as he could from this angle. "I barely got a chance to feel you before."

Oh my God. You can feel me like this as long as you want.

I put my hand over his on my hip, and he separated his fingers to let me curl mine between them as our bodies moved together. This wasn't the frantic pursuit of an orgasm. I couldn't put my finger on the rhythm or define the motion. Thrusting? Not really. It wasn't slow and gentle, it wasn't hard and fast, but somewhere in between, falling into perfect time with the warm breaths rushing past my neck. An orgasm was inevitable, but he was in no more of a hurry to give it to me than I was to give in to it. I rode that edge, and he rode me, and I couldn't remember... hell, I couldn't remember anything that wasn't happening right now in this room, in this bed.

I bit my lip and shuddered, my whole body tingling as his cock slid across my prostate at the most perfect angle, and suddenly I wanted to come so bad I was going to go insane, but the way he fucked me was *so* good, and the way he kissed my neck and breathed against my skin made every inch of my flesh break out in goose bumps. I wanted to come, but I didn't want to come because I didn't want this to end.

Something changed. I couldn't tell if he'd sped up, if he was fucking me harder, if he'd pushed himself deeper, or if my overwhelmed senses had finally just had enough and couldn't rein in the intensity anymore. I gripped his hand tighter. I didn't want to let go of him to stroke myself into that inevitable delirium, and I couldn't move to rock back against him and force him to take me over the edge—I could only lie there and bury my face in the pillow and nearly sob from the powerful sensations crashing through me. I was passive, I was helpless, and the only thing in the world left for me to do was to surrender, and when I did, the entire world shattered around me.

Ryan's fingers tightened between mine, digging almost painfully into my hip above my cast as he buried his face in my neck, and now he *was* thrusting, forcing his cock in deep. And then he was all the way inside me,

holding my body against his and pressing, grinding, trying to get even deeper as he shuddered, swearing just behind my ear. He released a sharp breath, tensed, and then
relaxed against me, resting his forehead on my shoulder.

"Oh… my God."

I reached back to stroke his hair. "My sentiments
exactly."

He laughed almost soundlessly and kissed the side
of my neck. Then he rested a hand on my hip and slowly withdrew, both of us gasping in that instant we physically separated. Neither of us moved for a moment.
I wasn't sure either of us even breathed. My whole
body was still tingling, and God only knew how overwhelmed he must have been if that was only the second
time he'd ever fucked anyone.

"Just so you know," he murmured, his lips brushing my ear, "this could get really addictive."

"You're telling me?"

I turned my head, and he found my lips with his
for a quick kiss.

"I'll be right back," he said, and got up. Once we'd
cleaned ourselves off, I lay on my back, and Ryan arranged the pillows under my cast. Then he lay beside
me, facing me.

"Do you want to stay here?" I asked. "For the
night?"

Ryan smiled. "I'd love to."

We settled in together. I turned onto my side again.
We arranged the pillows—again—to prop up my leg,
and then Ryan slid in behind me. We were both naked
and still, skin to skin, holding each other in a sleepy
pantomime of the way we'd fucked.

And lying like that, with Ryan's body against mine
and his arm draped over my waist, I drifted off to sleep.

CHAPTER THIRTEEN

RYAN WAS right. The sex we had was addictive. One taste and we were both hooked. If we weren't working, we were together, and if we weren't at the barn or grabbing a bite to eat, we were in bed. He was insatiable, and so was I, in spite of the constant headache and limited positions that came with fucking while half-wrapped in plaster. I could only imagine how insane things would get once the casts were gone.

Though we both had to work, it wasn't unusual at all for us to stay up way, way too late in one of our bedrooms. Whenever I came into work bleary-eyed and clinging to a coffee cup, Mike just shook his head and laughed. He'd done the same damned thing when he'd first started seeing Jason, so he kept his trap shut.

And then there were the weekends. The lazy mornings like this one when an alarm didn't go off and neither of us had to be anywhere.

Barely awake, I adjusted my position, trying to get comfortable without actually rolling over. That would have required me to wake up completely to rearrange my leg and pillows, so I tried to make do with only moving a little.

Beside me, Ryan stirred, and a second later his naked skin warmed mine as he draped his arm over my waist. His breathing was slow and soft against my neck. He was probably still asleep.

I put my hand over his and sighed, relaxing in his arms as I hovered between going back to sleep and waking up completely. Probably waking up. My awareness was expanding beyond the places we were making contact, and my muscles and joints were reminding me of their existence. My body ached all over, and it had nothing to do with the casts. It also wasn't remotely unpleasant, every twinge reminding me of the rough grasp or deep thrust that had created it.

Ryan stirred again. "You're awake."

"So are you."

"Mm-hmm." He nuzzled the back of my neck, his goatee tickling my skin. "I'd mention that last night was amazing," he murmured sleepily, "but that would be stating the obvious."

"Mmm, you're more than welcome to mention it, though."

"All right." He laughed and kissed below my hair. "Last night was amazing."

"I know. I was there."

Another soft laugh. "I don't suppose," he said between kisses beneath my ear, "you'd be opposed to switching one of these nights, would you?"

I bit my lip as a shiver went through me. "Not opposed in the slightest. All you have to do is say the word."

"I've been thinking about it for a while. Haven't quite worked up the nerve, but when I do…." He planted a lingering kiss below my jaw. "You'll be the first to know."

"I can't wait."

After we'd both gotten dressed, I walked—okay, hobbled—out to the living room with him to see him off. As soon as the door had shut, I closed my eyes and smiled to myself.

When I turned around to head into the kitchen for a much-needed cup of coffee, Brad was standing in the doorway, mug in hand, staring at me.

I cleared my throat, pretending that intense warmth wasn't rushing into my cheeks. "What?"

"What do you mean, what?"

"I mean why are you looking at me like that?"

He rolled his eyes. "Come on. Don't play stupid with me. I know you way too well."

"Oh, please." I made a dismissive gesture and headed into the kitchen to find some coffee. "He's hardly the first guy I've brought home since you've been here."

"Oh, no, it's not that." He rested his hip against the counter while I pulled a mug out of the cabinet. "I knew when I moved in not to hang anything breakable on the wall between our rooms because you'd probably knock it off with your headboard."

I laughed, focusing on pouring my coffee rather than meeting his eyes. "Err, sorry. Occupational hazard when you move in with a manwhore."

"Uh-huh."

"So why the weird look?"

"Besides the fact that you've been bringing the same guy home for weeks?" Brad set his coffee cup on the counter and eyed me. "Because of that silly grin you were wearing when you came in here."

"The… what? No!"

"Uh-huh. I know what I saw."

I shook my head. "There's nothing going on. It's just…." No, calling this *just sex* seemed disingenuous. "I mean, one thing…." No, one thing most certainly did not just lead to another, not even the first time. "There is nothing…." *Nathan, shut up.*

Brad laughed. "You are positively adorable when you're flustered like this."

I didn't laugh. My stomach fluttered, and it wasn't because of the butterflies Ryan kept causing. I focused on pouring and polluting my coffee instead, though I wasn't so sure my gut would let me drink any of it at this point.

Brad's laughter turned to an exasperated sigh. "You're fighting it hard, aren't you?"

"I'm not."

"Yeah. Okay."

I rolled my eyes. "Okay, fine. But you'd fight it too if—" My teeth snapped together.

"If?" He inclined his head.

I shifted my gaze from him to my coffee cup. "I was going to say if you'd been through the shit I have, but you're…."

"I'm not going through the same thing," he said.

"No, but… I didn't mean to downplay what you're dealing with."

"You didn't." He shrugged. "They're not the same. Jeff didn't hurt me. We just fell apart, and it's as much my fault as it is his."

I took a sip of coffee and finally faced him. "And you guys had something really good, but now you're… well, you're here. Can you see why I'm not all that encouraged to get involved with someone again?"

"Of course." He sipped his own coffee and set the cup aside again. "To tell you the truth, if Jeff and I really do call it quits, I'll probably take a break from the whole dating thing for a while myself."

"See? So you know exactly what I mean."

"I do. But I also know that if someone comes along, I'd rather fall on my face with him than regret letting something good pass me by."

I rolled some coffee around on my tongue.

"Whatever's happening between you two, Nathan, don't fight it." His voice was gentle. "I know you're afraid of someone stomping on you like that asshole did—"

"Like those *two* assholes did."

"Right. I get it. But this could really be something if you let it."

"It's fine the way it is," I said. "He's good company. He's fun in bed. Why ruin it by turning it into something it's not?"

"Because things like that have a tendency to evolve on their own, whether you like it or not."

I shook my head. "No. I'm done with that shit for a few years. Besides, he's leaving Tucker Springs in November. It doesn't have time to—"

"Nathan, mi amigo, I'm going to warn you right now: do not tell yourself he's safe because he's leaving in a few months."

My stomach flipped. "What do you mean?"

"I mean I know you, and I know how that little brain of yours works. You're thinking you can fuck around with this guy and have a good time, and you won't get attached because you *can't* get attached." Brad shook his head. "It doesn't work that way."

"Except what's the point of getting attached to someone who isn't going to stick around?" I half shrugged. "Even if I do get all starry-eyed over him and let myself think things are getting serious, this is a guy who's flat out said he won't commit to anything more than a tattoo." I gestured dismissively. "The guy can't stay in one place for more than a year or two. He's not going to let me tie him down, and I wouldn't want to tie him down."

"None of that means you won't get attached to him, though."

"I won't."

He held my gaze, then shrugged. "Okay. Just be careful with this guy, all right?"

"I will."

Though I would never have admitted it out loud, never mind directly to him, Brad's comments had rattled me. What if he was right? Ryan was amazing, but I wasn't at all ready for a relationship. Particularly not with someone who wasn't long for this town.

I was batting oh-for-two when it came to relationships. I'd only had two serious ones, and they'd both ended in excruciating disaster. Someday, yes, I wanted to fall in love and have a long-term relationship with someone, but not yet. I needed to mature some more. The dating pool needed to mature some more so I could date men my own age without feeling like we were both two dumb kids with no clue how this shit worked.

Someday. But not today.

And not Ryan.

I WATCHED Ryan from the bleachers. He had the sitting trot down, but I made him do it anyway. It was good for Tsarina. Good for him. And goddamn, it was good for me because he made it seem so effortless and gorgeous. He'd definitely gotten the hang of correct posture, that balance between staying still in the saddle but also moving with her, which meant a solid, tight core. As she floated around the arena in a steady, easy trot, his abs must have been gorgeous underneath his black T-shirt.

Much as I hated the way the summers here could get blistering hot, I secretly hoped this year was a scorcher. Then maybe he'd have to ride without a shirt on, and I could see if he was using his abs the way he was supposed to. For training purposes, of course.

I cleared my throat and called out, "Go ahead and walk her. Let her cool down for a few minutes." *Her and me both.*

He didn't make a sound or any obvious movements, but Tsarina made a smooth, flawless shift from a trot to a walk. They walked for a little while, Tsarina stretching her neck while Ryan reached down to pat and praise her.

Once she'd caught her breath, he reined her to a gentle halt. He swung his leg over the saddle and dropped onto the soft ground, landing on both feet. And I might have stolen a lingering glance while his back was turned. What could I say? The only thing hotter than perfectly relaxed-fit jeans on an ass like that was those jeans covered in dust.

I lifted my busted ass off the bleachers and hobbled into the barn behind them. Ryan put Tsarina on the crossties, and I sat on the tack trunk like I always did.

"I don't even know why you want lessons," I said as Ryan slipped Tsarina's bridle off. "You're a natural at this."

"Yeah, but you know the finer points." He eased the bit out of her mouth so it didn't clank against her teeth. Bridle in hand, he turned around. Perspiration darkened the edges of his hair, and he had a muddy smear of dust mixed with sweat across his forehead. "I didn't have a clue about half this shit when we started."

And I didn't have a clue how hot you'd look in the saddle.

I muffled a cough. "Well, you're a fast learner, then."

He just smiled and continued unsaddling Tsarina. Once she was back in her stall, he hung her halter and lead rope on the door. Then he helped me to my feet, and we headed out to the parking area.

Halfway from the door to the truck, he slowed and tilted his head back. "Wow, it's a gorgeous night tonight."

I looked up. Though the barn lights were bright as hell, the stars were clearly visible, especially with no moon. "You're right. It is."

"Yep. Well." He glanced at his watch. "I guess I should probably get you home."

"I don't know," I said. "I kind of like being out of the house."

"Do you?" He shifted his gaze back up to the sky. "In that case, do you feel like going for a drive?"

"To…?"

His gaze slid toward me, and he grinned. "Do you trust me?"

I eyed him skeptically but then shrugged. "Oh hell. Why not?"

We got into the truck, and Ryan drove us out onto the interstate. He took one of the exits at the edge of town and followed the highway west. Straight ahead of us, the mountains cut a jagged, lightless silhouette against the stars, and that silhouette seemed to grow taller as we drove, a wall of teeth pushing the stars farther out of our reach.

Streetlights were fewer and farther between out here. So were houses, and eventually even the farms were behind us. The highway wound upward and became a two-lane road with faded yellow stripes down the center. After a while those disappeared too, and a few miles later so did the asphalt.

A mile or so past a half-dead gas station, he turned down a gravel road. The truck bumped and bounced along the uneven terrain, though to his credit, Ryan managed to avoid the really nasty potholes.

I gazed out at the dark ravine on the right and the steep mountainside on the left. There probably wasn't another soul for miles. "You're not going to dismember me and bury me out here, are you?"

Ryan laughed. "Not while you've got those damned casts on, no."

I threw him a glance. "You know, a simple 'no' would have sufficed. The qualifier about the casts wasn't necessary."

"Hey, I'm just saying." He shrugged and kept his eyes on the dusty road ahead of us. "Taking limbs apart is hard enough without a plaster casing around them."

I smirked. "But I can't exactly run away from you."

"Eh, still. I like to work smarter, not harder. Efficiency and all that."

"Efficiency?" I put my casted hand over my heart and sighed dramatically. "A man after my own heart." I paused. "I mean, you know, hopefully not after it for a meal or something."

Ryan laughed again and reached across the console. His hand came to rest on my leg, right above the edge of my cast. "I promise, I'm not going to do anything like that."

"I'm going to hold you to that."

"Understood."

He kept driving for another fifteen minutes or so and finally stopped in the middle of nowhere. The engine quieted and the lights went out, and I couldn't see a damned thing because it was dark and, well, there wasn't a damned thing out here. We were high up on a ridge, that much I could tell, and if the sun had been up, we'd have been able to see the mountain range extending in front of us and behind us like reptilian vertebrae.

Right now, though, with only the stars for light, all I could see was darkness and the distant glow of Tucker Springs and a couple of the smaller towns nearby.

"So," I said. "I'm assuming we're not here to go hiking."

"Not very far, no."

A strangled sound escaped my throat. "Ryan, I'm—"

"Relax." He squeezed my leg. "About ten steps. Fifteen, tops. I promise."

"All right. But no more than fifteen."

He laughed again but then glanced at my leg and pursed his lips. "Hmm. With some help, you think you can get into the bed of the truck?"

I threw him a playful glare. "Is this the part where you start sawing off my limbs?"

Ryan groaned and rolled his eyes. "Seriously? You really think I want to get blood all over that bed liner? That shit was expensive, you know."

"Oh. Well. Why didn't you say so?" I unbuckled my seat belt. "Apparently you just wanted to get me into bed."

He snorted. "That's it. Of course." Patting my leg, he added, "Come on."

I got out of the truck and went around the back of the bed as Ryan lowered the tailgate.

"Hold on for a second." He jumped onto the tailgate and picked up a couple of folded blankets I hadn't seen sitting on the side rail.

As he unfolded them and laid them across the bed, I said, "You came prepared, I see."

He glanced up from spreading the second blanket on top of the first. "I… well…."

I folded my arms as best I could with a crutch and a cast. "Ryan, did you plan this?"

"Uh." He looked down at the edge of the blanket in his hands, his expression as sheepish as a kid who'd been busted pawing through the cookie jar. "Maybe?"

I laughed. "As long as you promise not to chop me up."

"Scout's honor."

With Ryan's help, I managed to get onto the tailgate, and from there, onto the blankets he'd spread out across the bed.

"I feel like an old man," I muttered. "Could've sworn I used to be able to jump into the back of a pickup without thinking twice."

Ryan laughed and kissed my cheek. "I'm sure once the cast comes off you'll be able to leap tall pickups in a single bound again." He leaned forward and dragged something heavy and metallic across the truck bed. "Here. Put your foot up on this."

I pushed myself up onto my elbows to see what he was talking about, and he tapped the top of his toolbox. He helped me put my foot up. Then he joined me, lying back on the blanket with a wadded-up jacket as a pillow. I rested my head on his shoulder, and he rested his hand on my arm.

With any other guy, I would've been sure we'd come up here to "park." That the stars and the silence were just convenient excuses to drive up into the mountains where no one would disturb us.

But Ryan didn't make a move beyond putting his arm around me. For the longest time we just lay there, gazing up at the sky.

I didn't know how much time passed before he finally broke the silence. "This is one of the things I love about Tucker Springs." His fingers ran back and forth along the edge of my sleeve as he stared up at the sky. "You don't have to drive very far to see the sky like this."

"I guess you don't, do you?"

"Nope. You know, I once heard there was a blackout in Los Angeles, and people suddenly started freaking out about these weird glowing clouds in the sky. Turned out it was the first time they'd ever seen the sky without all the light pollution, and what they were seeing was the Milky Way."

"Wow. You can really see the Milky Way?"

"If there's absolutely no light and it's perfectly clear? Yeah. And it's amazing." His fingers started moving again, slipping under my sleeve before trailing back and forth across my arm. "I don't know how true the LA story is, though. I mean, if you turned off every light in Southern California, you still have the smog to contend with. It has to be absolutely crystal clear to see that much."

"Like this?" I gestured up at the sky.

"A lot clearer and darker. Just imagine if there was no light pollution here at all."

"I don't see much all the way out here."

"It's pretty dark, but you've still got that little bit of a glow from the city." His fingers stopped moving, and he rested his hand on my arm. "You should see it when you get way out there in the middle of nowhere. Out in the desert or in the mountains without a single light for a hundred miles."

"I didn't think places like that still existed."

Ryan turned toward me and lowered his voice, almost whispering like we were conspiring instead of talking about stars. "You just have to know where to look."

"And you do know where to look?"

"Mm-hmm." He was quiet for a moment. "I was hoping for a night like this up in Canada once while I was camping, and ended up with the most amazing view of the northern lights instead."

"Ooh, I hear those are incredible in person."

"They are. That was one of the nights I wished I'd had someone with me, though."

"Oh yeah?" I turned a little, watching his nearly invisible profile. "Why's that?"

"It was so cool and so surreal," he said, his tone almost reverent. "I wished I'd had someone there to say 'yeah, this is really happening, and it really is this awesome.'"

I didn't know what to say to that. Silence fell again, and we both continued watching the sky.

Barely whispering, I broke the silence this time. "So do you think you'll ever settle down somewhere?"

He shrugged. "I don't know. There's never been a place that felt like home to me, you know?"

"Nowhere?"

"Nowhere." He absently ran his fingers up and down my arm. "On one hand, I think I could be happy just following the blacktop until I'm too old to keep going. On the other, part of me thinks I'm trying to find something, and I haven't found it yet."

"What are you trying to find?"

Eyes fixed on the sky above us, Ryan shook his head. "I don't know. I guess I figure when I find it, I'll know."

"And if you never do?"

Another shrug. "Then I will have spent my life doing a lot of cool shit and seeing a lot of cool things. And I've met some pretty amazing people along the way."

He turned toward me, so I mirrored him as best I could, and we faced each other in the darkness. Though I could barely see him in the low light, I could *feel* the way he was looking at me. And the way I was looking at him. There was something between us right then, some unspoken thing waiting in the corners and in the shadows for one of us to bring it out into the light. It was terrifyingly familiar, and at the same time intriguingly alien. Like a word on the tip of my tongue that I couldn't quite bring to life, but I'd know it the instant I heard it.

Secretly I hoped he'd be the one to break down and say it so we could give it a name. So I'd know what the hell I was feeling, and that he felt it too.

At the same time, I was afraid he *would* be the one to say it. That he'd breathe life into it and we wouldn't be able to pretend it didn't exist and things wouldn't stay the same.

He pushed himself up onto his elbow. "This wasn't… this wasn't why I brought you up here, but…."

"Better than chopping me up."

Ryan laughed. "I guess it is, isn't it?" The darkness between us shrank, and his lips were soft and cool against mine.

Some guys were all cologne and cleanliness, but right now Ryan was dust and leather and sweat and motor oil, nothing clean about him but purely masculine and, in some way I couldn't define, erotic. Like he was the sum total of everything that was raw and sexy, and I wanted nothing more than to get high off him. He teased my lips apart, and when I opened for him, he slipped his tongue past mine.

Then his hand drifted over the front of my shorts. I shivered, gripping his shoulder with my good hand as he squeezed me through my clothes.

"Fuck." I bit my lip and arched my back. "This… this why you brought me out here?"

"No." He kissed me as he started drawing down my zipper. "But now that we're here, it seems like a good idea."

"Yeah, it's… it's good. Keep…." My ability to speak vanished entirely as his warm fingers met my cock.

When he closed his hand and started stroking, I tried to thrust up against him, but the weight of my cast kept me pinned. I was completely helpless. Completely immobile and at his mercy with nowhere to go and no one to hear a thing, and that should have terrified me, but it didn't. I surrendered to it. Surrendered to *him*.

My hips moved of their own accord, pushing back against him as much my cast allowed, and the pressure

and the friction and his goddamned kiss were too intense. I broke the kiss with a gasp. I swore. Thought I
swore.

And suddenly the air above my lips was cool. Too
cool. But before I could make sense of it, Ryan's mouth
was on my cock, and I lost it, and they probably heard
me clear back in Tucker Springs as I came.

He was over me again, grinning, and I dragged him
down into a kiss. Tasting myself on his tongue, feeling
his weight on top of me, my whole body still tingling
from that orgasm…. I hadn't felt this amazing in a long,
long time.

"You know, when you get these casts off," he said
between kisses, "there's all kinds of things we could get
away with back at the barn."

Because that was what I needed: another reason
to want him to fuck me senseless *immediately*. "You
offering a literal roll in the hay?"

"Hmm, well, not the hay, but…." He kissed me
hard. "I could see myself fucking you up against the
tack room wall."

"Oh. God."

"That would be hot, wouldn't it? Especially if
there were—" He released a hot breath across my skin.
"—people around."

"You dirty bastard," I growled.

"Damn right. But that all has to wait until your
casts come off." He lifted up so I could see his face
in the low light. "Do you want to stay at my place tonight?" He smiled, and it *might* have passed for something innocent if not for that gleam in his eyes. "So
you don't have to go all the way up the stairs to your
apartment?"

I put my hand on his chest, barely keeping myself from grabbing a handful of his shirt. "Is that the only reason you want me to stay with you?"

"Well, not the *only* reason, no."

I grinned. "Don't bullshit me. This has nothing to do with the stairs up to my apartment, does it?"

"If I said it didn't, would you still come home with me?"

"My place is closer," I murmured. "And you're out of condoms, so we'd have to stop on the way."

"Hmm, damn. I don't want to make any stops. Guess we'll have to deal with the stairs, won't we?"

I didn't answer. I just pulled him down and kissed him.

And it was really happening.

And it really was that awesome.

CHAPTER FOURTEEN

MY BEDROOM was dark, and we were silent. No words. No moans or attempts at cursing. The only sounds besides our breathing—when we remembered to breathe at all—were hands moving on skin and skin moving on sheets.

Even the two casts didn't interfere much this time; we had long since grown accustomed to working around them without losing our stride. Not that we were in a big hurry tonight anyway. We were both naked, and hard, and panting between kisses, but everything we did was still slow and languid as if we had all night to get from here to orgasm.

"I want to switch," he murmured after a while. "Tonight."

One shudder, and all the breath left my lungs. "You do?"

He nodded.

I moistened my lips. "Except I still can't move much."

Ryan grinned against my lips. "Didn't say you had to move."

"Good, because I *can't* move."

"Don't worry about it." He kissed me once more. "I can get on top."

I shivered with anticipation. "Before you do, get me some lube."

Ryan grabbed the bottle from the nightstand. Then he straddled me, and once he was on top, I had him pour some on my first two fingers.

I grinned up at him. "Still on top, even on the bottom, huh?"

Chuckling, he leaned down to kiss me. "Well, when your cast comes off, we can negotiate some other positions."

"Hmm, I suppose we can." I ran my dry pinkie finger up his side to make him shiver. "When I can move and you can't."

"I'm looking forward to it," he growled, and claimed a demanding kiss.

So am I, Ryan. So am I.

I slid a hand between us. He groaned softly into my kiss as I ran the backs of my fingers along the underside of his cock and then over his balls, and when I continued downward, he gasped.

"If you want to stop," I said, "just say so."

Ryan nodded. He bit his lip as I found his entrance with a lubricated fingertip.

"Breathe," I whispered. "I'll go slow. I promise."

"Okay."

I pressed a fingertip in. He gasped. I eased my finger in slowly, a little at a time, and when he'd relaxed enough, I added a second.

Ryan's lips parted. He closed his eyes, twin creases forming between his eyebrows.

"Like that?" I asked.

"Uh-huh. My God...."

"Just wait," I said, my own anticipation bordering on unbearable. "Just you wait."

"I can't wait," he breathed. "I want... I want you to...."

"I will. Just have to take it slow. So I don't hurt you."

He bit his lip, the crevices between his eyebrows deepening. If he was anything like me, he was debating whether any pain that came would be worth skipping all of this and getting straight to taking my cock. And if he was anything like me, he was leaning very heavily toward deciding that yes, it was worth it, *come on and fuck me already*.

I slid both fingers a little deeper and bent them.

His eyes flew open. His lips parted again, but no sound or even breath came out.

I moved my hand faster, fucking him with my fingers, watching his eyes and remembering what it was like the first time someone had shown me why they call the prostate the male G-spot. The newness of the sensations, the sheer overwhelming pleasure—I'd never forgotten that feeling, and watching Ryan now, I could almost feel it again.

"F-fuck me," he whispered. "Oh my God... fuck... fuck me."

I slowly withdrew my fingers. "Get me a condom."

He reached for the drawer beside the bed, riffled around for a moment, and came back with a condom. He glanced down at my casted hand and smirked. "I'm guessing you'll need some help with this."

"It's either that or you have to wait until I figure out how to do it one-handed."

"In that case…." He tore the condom wrapper with his teeth.

We were both silent as he put the condom on me. Maybe he just needed to concentrate on the motions— putting a condom on someone else had tripped me up the first few times. Maybe he was too turned on, too focused. All I knew was having his hands on me, having him carefully rolling on the latex, killed any ability I had to speak. Fucking. That was all my mind had left. Fucking. Getting inside him for the first time.

I want to fuck you so bad, Ryan….

He picked up the lube I'd been using earlier, poured some into his hand, and stroked it onto my cock. I squirmed as he teased me through the condom.

"You want… you want me to fuck you?" I asked. "Or you want to make me come like this?"

Abruptly his hand stopped. "Well, when you put it like *that*…."

I swore under my breath. "Get on top. Now."

"I love it when you're bossy," he growled, and kissed me. Then, just before I was certain I was going to lose my mind, he got back on top and lifted himself up a little. I steadied my cock with my good hand.

"Easy," I whispered as he came down. "Go slowly."

He nodded and eased himself onto the head of my cock. A little more pressure, and we both gasped as the first inch or so slid into him. He was so goddamned tight, almost painfully so. He came up a little, then started down, but winced.

"Relax," I said. "Just breathe and take it slow. There's no… there's no rush."

Ryan licked his lips and closed his eyes as he came down again. As he took me deeper, I moved my hand to his hip. A little at a time, he took more, and he moved faster, and I didn't know how the hell I was going to last when I was this turned on. My hand slipped off his hip because I couldn't concentrate enough to hold on. I desperately wanted to grab him and thrust upward into him, but I couldn't do anything. All I could do was lie there and let him ride my cock at his own speed, taking every inch of me at the most agonizingly slow pace.

Somehow I found the concentration and coordination to move my hand, and I stroked his cock, keeping perfect time with his rhythm, and as he locked eyes with me, my heart skipped. Staring straight into his eyes, holding his gaze while he rode me, while I stroked him…. God, the things I felt. Being inside him and being close to orgasm weren't even the half of it.

What the hell is….

I have you, I'm inside you, but I still want more. I want it—want you—so bad it hurts.

How do you have this effect on me?

What the actual hell?

Then he closed his eyes. His head fell forward, and his lips moved soundlessly. His cock got harder in my hand, so I stroked him a little faster, and his rhythm faltered but he kept riding me anyway. When he bit his lip and whimpered and came on my stomach, I couldn't hold back anymore. My whole body was shaking, my toes curling as much as the plaster allowed, and my back arched as I came inside him.

Panting hard, he sank down to me and kissed me. "Even better… than I thought it would be."

I grinned against his lips but was too out of breath and too overwhelmed to speak, so I kissed him again.

He lifted himself off me. Even with one hand, I managed to get the condom off, and with a little help from my cast hand, tied it and tossed it into the trash beside the bed.

Then he joined me again, and we wrapped ourselves up in a gentle, lazy embrace and a lazier kiss. I loved the way he felt against me like this. Loved the taste of his kiss and the heat of his skin against mine.

And I still couldn't shake the way I'd felt when I'd looked up at him, looked right into his eyes as we'd both inched toward orgasm.

That hadn't been just lust, and I couldn't convince myself otherwise. It was far too deep and terrifying and visceral to be lust alone.

How the hell had we gotten to this point? I'd sworn it wouldn't happen. Was Brad really right? *Fuck.* It had been too easy. Effortless. We'd slipped into this so subtly, I hadn't noticed until we were in this deep.

I couldn't. I just… I couldn't. Ryan would be gone before winter, and my past still stung. Back-to-back disastrous relationships—the rebound being an even more colossal failure than the one I'd been rebounding from—had left me jaded, and both of those wounds were still raw.

So what the fuck did I do now?

WHEN I awoke, Ryan was gone. In my half-conscious state, I almost panicked, but then I heard the distinctive swish of someone rinsing a razor in water across the hall.

I sat up, grumbling and cursing as I maneuvered my non-bendy leg from bed to floor.

Ryan leaned in through the bedroom doorway, one side of his face still white with shaving foam. "Oh, hey. I didn't wake you, did I?"

"No, not at all." I sat up slowly. Man, I missed being able to stumble out of bed without navigating around a bunch of plaster. Soon, though. Very soon.

"Okay. Good." He gestured with the razor in his hand. "Let me finish up. I'll be back in a second."

"Take your time," I said as he disappeared into the bathroom. Pity I couldn't see him from here. Nothing quite like watching a man shave.

I shook my head and reached for my crutch.

"Need a hand?" he called from the bathroom.

"Not yet, but in a minute."

"Be right there." The faucet turned on and the razor swished in the water again.

We'd gotten this morning routine down pat. Ryan helped me with anything I couldn't do, and he patiently waited while everything else—brushing my teeth, getting dressed—took twice as long as it normally would have. We'd probably be confused and wouldn't know what to do with ourselves when next week came along, the casts came off, and I could handle mundane tasks at my usual speed.

And none of that helped unwind this knot in my stomach. Getting into a comfortable, domestic routine, not batting an eye at my constant dependence—that wasn't how things were supposed to be between us. When the hell had this happened? I had to figure out how to take us back a few steps. Back to what we were supposed to be, not... not this.

Dressed, shaved, ready for work, we stood in the bedroom.

"I guess we should get going," he said.

"Yeah. Bosses might not be happy if we're late."

But we didn't move. And the way he looked at me right then was unsettling, especially the way it roused the butterflies in my stomach and made my heart beat in a way it only had a few times in my life. The way it had last night while we'd made—

Fucked. While we'd *fucked*.

He cupped my face tenderly. I shivered, knowing damn well a kiss would be a bad idea right now because his eyes didn't say *I guess we should get going*.

"We should…." I let my gaze flick toward his lips, then back up to his eyes. "We…."

Ryan kissed me. His kisses had lost that tentative uncertainty from the beginning—he was completely confident now, totally sure of himself as he took us from a soft goodbye kiss to something that was definitely… not. Not soft. Not goodbye.

"You're going to be late for work," I said, though I made no move to separate myself from him.

"I'm always on time." His hand drifted down my waist. "I can be a few minutes late this one time."

He'd be more than a few minutes late. A few minutes would have accounted for a feverish half-dressed quickie, a promise of more, and a kiss goodbye. Not a long, languid fuck, clothes on the floor and Ryan on top of me, taking me with perfect slow strokes until I came inside him. Not me lying on the edge of the bed and finishing him off with a long, drawn-out blow job while he stood gripping the bedpost for balance. Not him reminding me with every touch why making love was even hotter than an all-out fuck.

And definitely not the long, gentle kiss. Or the longer, blissful look before a whispered "we should get out of bed" led to one more—just *one* more—kiss. And then one more.

It was sensual. It was perfect.

It fucking terrified me.

"Let me guess: if he comes along at the wrong time, he can't possibly be Mr. Right?"

"Something like that."

And besides, how could I fall for someone who couldn't see a horizon without seeing something he needed to keep on chasing? That was a recipe for disaster.

"Mark my words, kid." Brad's comments echoed in the back of my mind like an ominous prophecy. *"You don't want him, which is exactly why he's going to show up."*

Oh, I wanted him all right, except it wasn't only the timing that was wrong. Even if Ryan had shown up a year from now, or five years from now, the fact remained that I couldn't let myself fall in love with a flight risk.

And right now I can't fall in love with anyone.

Something had to give. Maybe we just needed to talk it over. Get on the same page. If he didn't like to tie himself down to anything, then he'd understand, wouldn't he? This was probably all in my head. If I was balking at the idea of this being more than sex-'til-November, then he probably felt the same way.

Ryan lifted himself up and met my eyes. "You okay? You seem kind of… elsewhere all of a sudden."

I broke eye contact, watching my fingers trace the edges of his tattoo.

"Nathan?" He turned my chin so I had very little choice but to look at him. "Just talk to me."

I tried to hold his gaze, but that reminded me of the way we'd held each other's gazes while we'd fucked—*still can't admit that was making love, can you?*—and I broke eye contact. "I need to know what we're doing."

"What do you mean?"

"I mean, we started out as friends. Then we started sleeping together. But we've never really talked about… about if it's only sex, or…."

"Or more?"

I nodded. "Yeah."

"What do you think?" he asked. "Do you think what we're doing… is it…."

His hopeful tone made my stomach want to fold in on itself.

Oh God. Oh God, no, let's not go there.

I gulped. "Is it what?"

Ryan shrugged, avoiding my eyes. "I'm not even sure. I've dated a few guys here and there, fooled around a little, but this…." He lifted his gaze again. "This seems different."

No. No, no, no…. Ryan….

"It does," I admitted. "But does that—"

"If you're asking if I have feelings for you beyond sex," he said quickly, "the answer is yes."

Fuck. Damn it.

"You… really?"

He nodded, some color blooming in his cheeks. The way he slowly pulled in a breath, I knew what was coming. I knew damn well what was coming. I could almost hear the words already ringing in my ears.

"Wait." I put a hand on his chest. "I'm…. Ryan, I can't."

He blinked. "What?"

"I'm sorry. I can't do this. Sex is fine, but I can't give you anything beyond that. Not… not now."

He pulled back a little, slowly releasing his breath. "Oh."

"I'm sorry. I've just had—"

"To be honest," he broke in, his tone cold as he sat up, "I'm not really interested in why."

I swallowed. "Uh. Okay."

"If you don't want to do this, then…." He shrugged, his taut expression chipping away at his indifferent exterior. "Then let's call it off and move on."

I stared at him. I had no idea what to say to that.

He leaned down and picked up his shirt. "I'm going to go."

I was still speechless. Things like this usually ended with screaming and with slamming doors, or at least some emotional pleading and arguing, and I didn't understand this. I didn't know what to make of his abrupt, quiet—if chilly—acceptance.

Ryan stood and picked up his clothes. He pulled on his jeans but carried his shoes and his shirt, and he also didn't fully turn around as he spoke over his shoulder. "Take care, Nathan."

"Yeah. I will. Uh, you too."

"I will."

And just like that, without a single protest or *But are you sure?* he was gone. Just… gone. Out the bedroom door, down the hall, out of my apartment, and down those stairs that he'd helped me up and down so fucking many times. I didn't hear the truck, but after a few minutes had passed, I was pretty sure if I looked outside, I wouldn't see that old black pickup in the guest spot.

I rubbed a hand over my face and cursed under my breath. This shouldn't have happened that fast. Ripping off the bandage was sometimes the most painless thing, but this should have been... I didn't know. Slower? More drawn out? It had ended too quickly. Too simply. Far too abruptly. It seemed unfinished, though it was definitely finished.

Ryan was gone. Of course he was. I'd awkwardly and not very eloquently told him what I should have told him a dozen fucks ago. Before things had had a chance to get this far. I'd finally said it, and now he was gone. I'd thought maybe we could be friends or something, but....

"If you don't want to do this, then let's call it off and move on."

This was how it had to be. Sooner or later Ryan would get restless and leave Tucker Springs, which meant that no matter how this conversation had gone, sooner or later he'd be gone. Better to let him go now before I became either something he left behind or something he resented for keeping him here.

"To be honest, I'm not really interested in why."

Deep breath. Stiff upper lip. Ryan was gone because I needed him to be, and eventually I'd get over him. I had to. I couldn't do this right now no matter how much I liked him.

I sighed and closed my eyes.

Self-preservation could be a real bitch sometimes.

CHAPTER FIFTEEN

NOTHING HAD ever been as liberating as the moment the cast came off my leg. I couldn't move my leg much, and none of the soft tissue was interested in bending or anything crazy like that, but having the damned thing off was like being released from a ball and chain.

Minutes later the second one was off too. I gingerly flexed my fingers for the first time in almost twelve weeks. Ahh, *freedom*.

I couldn't walk without limping, but at least I could *walk*. The joints were stiff, the muscles aching furiously now that they had to work again, but whatever. Just being out of that cast meant freedom.

I left the doctor's office and drove straight to the barn. The excitement in my stomach rivaled the first time I'd gone to ride Tsarina after I'd bought her, though hopefully this time would have a better outcome.

It didn't help that I hadn't been to see her in a week. Not since.... *Don't think about that day. Just don't.* I'd had Cody lunge her for me to keep her exercised, but I hadn't been here myself.

My boots—two this time, not one and a crutch—echoed weirdly as I walked down the aisle. The barn was full of activity. At least a dozen people were here to work their horses, and Cody and a few others were standing around talking.

Still, the place was eerily empty. Like something was missing.

"Tsarina?" I said as I approached her stall, and when her head appeared over the door—ears up and eyes wide—I couldn't help smiling. "Hey, sweetheart. You miss me?" I held out my hand with a treat on my palm, and she munched on that as I patted her neck.

A weird ball of apprehension formed in my stomach. I was here. I could walk and use both hands. Everything was back the way it needed to be.

I took her halter off the hook and unbuckled it. When the buckle jingled, I froze. I'd heard that sound hundreds of times over the years, but this time it brought to mind a familiar pair of hands maneuvering the strap through the buckle. The phantom vibration of a low, playful voice talking to Tsarina while the halter slipped onto her head.

And that was when the lump rose in my throat. Ryan's absence was suddenly as conspicuous as the missing cast around my leg and completely incongruous in this place. He had become as much a fixture in this barn as the country music playing in the background and the cats wandering the rafters.

I put the halter back on the hook.

I had told myself all week that I'd stayed away because I couldn't ride or groom Tsarina. Being able to see her but not do anything beyond petting her over the door was too damned frustrating, so in spite of my guilt, I'd avoided the barn and promised myself I'd make up for it once the casts were off.

But now the casts were off and I was here, and the guilt burned deeper because Tsarina hadn't been the one I'd been avoiding after all.

I missed the easy banter. I missed watching Ryan play with Tsarina while she stood in the crossties. Teasing her with the end of a whip as she tried to eat it. Laughing at the faces she made when he scratched her withers. Carefully putting on her bridle so he could ride her.

I cleared my throat and patted Tsarina's neck. I'd come back another night. I wasn't ready to ride yet anyway. Not for at least a couple of weeks, until I'd regained some of the strength in my leg. Maybe sooner than that, according to the doctor, but caution would keep me on the ground until I was absolutely sure I was ready.

Not afraid to get back on, are you?

I shook away that thought and walked faster toward my car. The incident with Tsarina wasn't the first time I'd been thrown. The first time the horse had come down with me, yes, and the first time I'd broken any bones, but I'd been unloaded a few times before.

Except after every one of those falls, I'd been able to get up and get right back on. The harder the fall, the longer it took to catch my breath and get my wits about me, but damn it, I'd always gotten back on.

Always, except this last time. Now weeks had gone by. The fear had had a chance to cool, but instead it had simmered below the surface, burning itself deeper beneath my skin while my leg healed.

And it still needed to heal a little, I reminded myself. The connective tissue was stiff and the muscles were atrophied, and I couldn't ride if I couldn't use my leg. Or my hand, for that matter. I needed to let my leg heal a bit more. I needed a little more time.

I needed to get the fuck out of here.

STANDING ON the ground floor of my apartment building, I stared at the steps for a moment, psyching myself up. No crutch this time. No cast.

I've got this.

I took a deep breath and started upward. It was a slow process, my muscles getting exhausted after a few steps, but eventually I made it to the top on my own.

When I cleared the top step, the sense of triumph was short-lived. I caught myself searching for the person who'd helped me to the top, and though Ryan hadn't been the only one to help me—hadn't been there at all in the past week—I half expected to see him standing there.

This was so weird. It wasn't like I was incapable of being alone. I wasn't solitary by nature, but I liked having some time to myself. I liked driving around alone. I didn't need to have someone with me all the time.

But Ryan's absence was so conspicuous, I couldn't avoid it. I couldn't get used to it the way I had the casts I'd finally gotten rid of. Those had been annoyances whenever they'd gotten in my way, but I could forget about them from time to time when I wasn't trying to move around.

Ryan's absence was more like a paper cut. Constantly there. Constantly stinging so I couldn't ever be unaware of it.

I blew out a breath and shook my head.

I'd recovered from the broken leg and the broken hand, and I'd recover from this. Just because the wound was still fresh and still hurt didn't mean it wouldn't heal.

As I let myself into the apartment, Brad looked up from the recliner where he sat.

"Hey, hey!" He clicked off the TV and grinned broadly at me. "Not the bionic man anymore, eh?"

"Bionic, my ass," I grumbled. "I couldn't move for shit."

"I think that's the idea of a cast. You know, gives the bones a chance to heal before your dumb ass gets hurt again?"

"True. But still."

"Well, glad to see you up and around now."

"Thanks."

He smiled but then turned serious. "So, um, thought I should mention this sooner than later, but I'm probably going to be getting my own place pretty soon. Since I'll be on my own for a while, I figured I should give you your space back."

My heart sank. "You and Jeff decided to call it quits?"

"Well, not exactly."

"What do you mean?"

"We're going to start over. From the beginning. Start dating each other again and see if we can work our way back to what it was before. You know, without fucking it up again."

"Good. Good to hear." I forced a smile. "I hope you guys can get back on your feet."

"Me too. Scared the hell out of me there for a while. I thought things were going to fall apart completely."

"Yeah, I was worried about you guys."

"Well, we're not out of the woods yet, but... I feel a lot better now that we're trying again."

"I can imagine."

"Guess we'll see how it goes." He gestured at the kitchen. "I was going to make some chicken tonight. You want any?"

"Sure, I could eat."

As we ate in front of the TV, I couldn't follow the show. My mind kept wandering back to the barn and to the empty, unsettling feeling that had followed me around since then. Truth be told, I'd been a space case ever since Ryan had left for the last time, but I'd convinced myself it was the same shit that had been distracting me for the past twelve weeks: trying to go about my business with heavy blocks of plaster imped-ing even the simplest tasks.

But those blocks were gone now.

And so was Ryan.

Brad waved a hand in front of my face. "Hey. You all right?"

I sighed. "I don't think so."

He sat beside me on the couch. "What's wrong?"

"Ryan." I took a deep breath, suddenly struggling to keep my composure. "I can't stop thinking about him." I rubbed a hand over my face. "I can't sleep. I can't think at work. Today I barely remembered how to drive. I'm... I'm a fucking mess."

"Think maybe that's because calling it quits was a mistake?"

I shook my head. "No. If it's this bad now, think how bad it would be when he left in November."

"Unless you guys did a long-distance relationship."

"Not that it matters. We're not doing any kind of relationship now." I rubbed my eyes. "Fuck…."

"Nathan, I think—"

"Please don't say I told you so. I get it. You were right. I got in over my head with Ryan."

"That wasn't what I was going to say." He squeezed my shoulder. "But you've been a wreck for a week, so maybe you should talk to him. See if there's any way to fix this."

I shook my head. "He didn't want to hear why I was ending things. I don't think he'll want to hear why I think I fucked up."

"Maybe he will, maybe he won't." Brad's hand was heavy on my shoulder. "But I think he means way too much to you to just wallow in this and hope it all goes away. It's not going to."

I kept my gaze down.

Brad drew his hand back. "You remember what it was like when things ended with Steve?"

I groaned. "God. Do I ever. Cheating asshole…."

"And how did it feel when you left Brent?"

"It was a relief. He was an asshole, and it was long overdue."

"But you were still angry."

"Of course I was. I wasted a year of my life with that fuckwit."

Brad nodded slowly. "Right. So when Steve left, you were angry and hurt, and you never wanted to see his idiot ass again. When Brent left, you felt like you'd gotten your life back." Brad reached over and put a hand on my arm. "How do you feel now?"

My shoulders sank. As an ache rose in my throat, my vision blurred.

And that was the moment I knew I'd really fucked up. That letting Ryan go—no, kicking him to the curb—had been a huge mistake. Because right then, I did what I hadn't done when Steve and Brent exited stage left: I cried.

I couldn't even tell myself it was simply the pent-up frustration from being dependent and unable to do the simplest tasks on my own for three long months. No, that had pissed me off, but this hurt. Straight to the bone.

Brad put his arms around me. "I know it hurts. I could see it the second you walked in."

I wiped my eyes but couldn't quite bring myself to speak.

"Give him a call." Brad let me go but kept a hand on my shoulder. "Tell him you made a mistake, and apologize."

"And if he doesn't want to hear from me?"

"You can't force him," Brad admitted softly. "But nothing's going to happen unless you at least give it a try. You fell hard for this guy in spite of trying your damnedest not to. That means whatever there was between you two, it's worth the effort and the risk to save it."

I wiped my eyes again. "Okay. I'll talk to him."

"That's all you can do." Brad hugged me again, a little tighter this time. "Good luck."

"Thanks. You too."

"Thanks. We'll probably need it."

"So will I."

CHAPTER SIXTEEN

FOR THE hundredth time, I pulled up Ryan on my phone and let my thumb hover over the Send button.

And for the hundredth time, I chickened out.

Fear kept me off the phone. All I heard over and over was Brad saying "You can't force him," and I was scared to death of the click and the silence on the other end of the line. I was terrified to hear Ryan push me away, even if I totally deserved it.

After three days, though, I couldn't take it anymore.

Fuck pride. Fuck fear. There was no way this situation was changing unless I changed it, because Ryan sure as hell wasn't going to magically appear on my doorstep to beg me to come back, and sitting here pitying myself wasn't doing anybody any good.

Before I could talk myself out of it, I grabbed my keys and left the apartment. I couldn't call. It would have been too easy for one or both of us to hang up if things got heated. He could ignore—or block—my number. Besides, some things couldn't be dealt with over the phone. I needed him to see me look him in the eyes and tell him I was sorry and how I felt about him.

The drive from my place to his seemed to drag on for hours. Several times I considered turning around—what was the point of hashing all this out again?—but made myself keep going. With my heart in my throat, I pulled up to Ryan's apartment building and parked in a guest spot.

His truck was out front. That was promising.

I took a deep breath before getting out of the car. On the way up the walk, I almost turned back. Twice. The short walkway—one of the perks of going to his place back when I'd been unable to walk very far—didn't give me too many opportunities for hesitation, though, and I made myself get all the way to his door.

I knocked.

No answer.

After almost a minute, I tried again.

Still nothing.

Crap. Now what?

Now you get the fuck out of here, because he obviously doesn't want to see you.

Heart heavy, I headed back to the car. I paused at the door, debating sending him a text, or calling him, or coming back later. Something told me I had one chance at contact, and if I couldn't fix this before he broke that contact, then it was done.

And if I walked away now, would I ever work up the nerve to come back?

Maybe I should let it go before either of us has a chance to say something to make this really *hurt.*

Before I could make a decision one way or the other, the all-too-familiar sound of a motorcycle engine raised the hairs on the back of my neck.

Slowly I turned around. Now wasn't that a surreal and oddly familiar sight? The bike. The leathers. The helmet. Blue and white between streaks of mud. Just like the day I'd met him.

He parked beside his truck. The engine died. I gulped.

When he took off the helmet, his eyes were cold. He didn't say a word, but I sensed the *fuck off* from here.

"I want to talk," I said.

He regarded me silently for a moment. Then he shrugged. "Okay."

Well, that was a start.

He keyed us into the apartment and set the helmet on a chair by the door before he started taking off his leather jacket, the same one he'd left with me when he'd gone to get the paramedics.

"You got the casts off," he said flatly. "How is your leg? And your hand?"

"They're fine. A lot better now."

"Good." He paused. "You probably want to sit."

Truth was, my leg ached like hell, but I didn't want to overstay my already tenuous welcome. "It's up to you."

Without a word, he gestured toward the small living room. I sat on the couch. He stayed standing, which was unnerving. The height difference, the defensiveness in the way he folded his arms—I suspected he wouldn't have invited me to sit if I hadn't been in a cast recently.

I cleared my throat. "I, um, I wanted to tell you I'm sorry."

"You mentioned that the last time we talked."

"Yeah, but I didn't include the part where I was sorry because I'd made a huge mistake." I paused, taking a deep breath. "I really am sorry, Ryan. I got spooked, and I fucked up and hurt you. I am so, so sorry for that."

He was quiet for a long moment. Finally he spoke, his tone flat and even. "I can accept the apology. But I'm not going back."

My heart dropped. "Ryan...."

He shook his head. "I've been avoiding this kind of thing for years because I was happier on my own. Things were different with you, but...." He finished the thought with a heavy shrug.

"Yes, they were different." I paused again, collecting my breath and thoughts. I started to speak, but he beat me to the punch.

"Listen, it was fun while it lasted. Maybe it could have gone somewhere, maybe it couldn't have. But I need to move on."

"Move on?" I asked. "Is that how you deal with everything? Stay until things get rough, and then 'move on'?" *Pot... kettle....*

"I'm not the one who called time on this," he snapped, and I jumped at the uncharacteristic sharpness in his voice. "This was *your* decision, Nathan."

"And it was a mistake."

"Was it? So if we tried again, how long before you decide *that's* a mistake too?"

Sighing, I rubbed my forehead as I struggled to find the words to assure him that I didn't flip-flop on these things as a rule, and I knew damn well I'd made a mistake by leaving, not by coming back.

Ryan spoke first. "One day you can't do this. The next you can't do without. How do I know tomorrow I won't be back out on my ass? I mean, you had the nerve to ask if I deal with everything by moving on and running away from anything that might hurt, but I could ask you the same thing, couldn't I?"

I flinched. "I...."

"You've been hurt a few times, and you're scared of getting hurt again. So you're going to hang back and let life pass you by? Are you also going to sell Tsarina because of your leg?"

"That was an accident," I snapped.

"Yeah? So if you'd been on foot when I came around that corner, you still would have broken your leg?"

I avoided his eyes.

"I don't let people in very often," Ryan said. "Every time I do, I wind up getting used for something, whether it's a blow job now and then or the fact that I've conveniently got a car." He swallowed. "And the few times I've let someone in *twice*...." Trailing off, he broke eye contact. "I can't. I'm sorry."

"Ryan, listen to me," I pleaded, my voice shaking. "I was never using you. I got in deeper than I thought I would, and I got scared. I was trying to keep from getting hurt myself, and I can't apologize enough for hurting you."

"And how long before it happens again?" The anger in his tone faltered in favor of something less steady. He eased himself onto the couch a safe distance away from me. "I mean, maybe this all makes sense to you, but the only thing I know for sure is how it felt when it was over. And I don't want to feel like that again."

"I don't want to hurt you again either." I barely resisted the urge to reach for him, just to make some contact even though I knew damn well it wouldn't be welcome. "I didn't want to hurt you the first time. I was trying to keep myself from getting hurt. It was obviously a misguided attempt, but you were leaving soon and—"

"You're using the fact that I might leave Tucker Springs to justify all this shit?" He glared at me. "The fact that I'm not putting down roots in this town justifies the fact that *you* walked away from *me*?"

"No, not at all." I put up my hands. "Please, just let me finish. Hear me out."

Ryan set his jaw and narrowed his eyes but didn't say anything.

I took a breath. "If anything, I used the fact that you were leaving Tucker Springs to let my guard down. I figured since there didn't seem to be time for anything to happen between us, then it wouldn't. And I let myself get more involved with you than I thought I would. I thought since you were leaving, nothing would happen. But... it did. And it terrified me."

"So what you're saying is I was worth it to fuck for a while because you knew I'd eventually leave?"

"What? No."

His eyebrow arched.

"That's not... that's not...." I exhaled. "To be honest, I figured we were both just in it for a little while, and when you left, that would be it. I didn't think either of us would get this emotionally invested. It wasn't that I was using you and ignoring how you felt. It just seemed like we were both happy with sex and nothing more. I didn't... I didn't realize it would go this far."

"And yet when it did, your first instinct was to run."

"Once bitten," I said.

"Yeah. Once bitten is right."

I met his eyes again. "Okay, listen. I understand why you don't give out second chances. That's how I've been screwed over a few times too."

He watched me, but his expression didn't change. It was completely blank and unreadable, every card held tight against his vest.

I folded my hands to keep from wringing them. "Ryan, you've never done this before, and—"

"No, I haven't." He glared at me. "So what? Does that mean—"

"It means I know how bad it hurts when it falls apart."

"As do I," he growled.

"Yes, you do. God, Ryan, I'm sorry. I really am." I exhaled hard and ran a hand through my hair. "The thing is, I've been doing everything I can to avoid going through that again, even if it meant never letting anything get off the ground." I took a deep breath. "Even when I meet someone who's obviously worth the risk and who I managed to fuck over because I'm afraid of getting fucked over again."

Ryan's brow furrowed, but he didn't say anything.

I moistened my lips. "I've been through hell and back because of guys, and I was afraid to do that again."

"Did you think I would do that to you?"

"I didn't think the other guys would either."

He arched his eyebrow again. "And I didn't think you would."

I exhaled. "I—"

"Just because I'm inexperienced doesn't make me an idiot. I'm not going to set myself up to fall on my face again. And for that matter, look at it from where I'm standing. In the beginning, you told me I wasn't obligated to keep helping you out. But I never saw it that way. Everything I was doing was because I wanted to, not because I thought I was obligated or because I wanted to get into your pants. Yeah, I felt bad for what happened to you—and I still do—but I also started to… feel something. I liked you. I wanted to be with you. That had never happened to me before. With anyone." He locked eyes with me, the pain in his palpable even from where I sat. "But suddenly you're getting close to being able to function on your own again and I'm no longer needed?"

I blinked. "That's what you thought this was about? That I was pushing you aside because I was getting my independence back? Yes, I was desperate to get back on my own two feet, but that had nothing to do with you." I swallowed. "I was never in this to use you, Ryan."

"Then what *were* you in it for?" He wrung his hands in his lap, watching them rather than looking at me. "Because all I know is one minute I was attracted to you, the next I was feeling something stronger for you, and then I was out on my ass. Right when you didn't *need* me anymore."

"No, no, no." I sat straighter and faced him. "Honestly, it wasn't like that at all. Quite the opposite, actually."

He faced me and furrowed his brow but didn't speak.

"The last few months were…." I shook my head and sighed. "I don't do very well depending on people. I never have. That's been a really difficult thing to do even though I knew I had to, and with that on top of letting myself get involved with you, I was… overwhelmed, I guess. I told myself I wouldn't get emotionally invested in anyone for a while, but then I did, at the same time I had to depend on you, and Brad, and…." I

sighed again. "I hate feeling like I'm incapable of taking care of myself; having someone see me like that
from the beginning makes my skin crawl. But I never
felt like you thought I was weak or incapable. You never made me feel that way. And that—the fact that it was
always okay and never an imposition or a reason to pity
me—it made me feel that much more for you. And then
I got scared. And I left. And I'm so sorry I hurt you,
Ryan. I don't know how many ways I can say that."

Ryan lowered his gaze. Some of his defenses
seemed to come down too, his posture relaxing slightly,
but the distance between us remained.

I sat up a little, then rested my elbows on my knees.
"I told you about my roommate, right? About why he's
staying with me?"

Ryan nodded. "Because he and his boyfriend
split." The slight arch of his eyebrow asked exactly
how that was relevant.

"Yeah, they did. Sort of. Thing is, he and Jeff have
been together for years. The last year or so, things kind
of went to shit, and Brad left a few months ago. Moved
in with me until they could figure out what they were
doing."

"Okay…?" The arched eyebrow and its unspoken
question remained.

"They're trying again," I said. "They're not picking up where they left off and pretending everything
is perfect. They're starting at the beginning. Dating.
Working their way back toward what they had before."

Ryan shifted a little. "If they haven't been able to
work it out, then what's the point?"

"Because Brad thinks Jeff is worth going through
the effort and trying one last time," I said quietly. "And
Jeff thinks Brad is worth it." I paused. "And you and

I had only just started dating, but I'm here because I think you're worth it." I knew damn well I was leaving myself open for a retort of "You're not, get out," but I put it out there and hoped for the best.

Silence. More goddamned silence.

"That's all I have," I said softly.

"I really liked what we had," he said. "That was the first time I'd ever felt anything like that. For anyone. And when you walked away…." Trailing off, he shook his head. "I don't want to set myself up for that again."

"Neither do I. That's why I left. I… I freaked out." With a hell of a lot of effort, I met his eyes again. "You're not used to staying in one place very long. I'm not used to staying with one man. But if you'll give me—and Tucker Springs—another chance, maybe we can make this work." I moistened my lips. "This is new to me too, Ryan."

He cocked his head. "But you've had relationships before."

"Not like this one." Struggling to hold his gaze, I whispered, "I've never met anyone who made me feel like this."

His expression didn't change. His posture didn't budge. The panic in my gut grew, and with every silent second, I was certain he was one sudden move away from bolting. My opportunities to turn this around were dwindling fast, and if he got away this time, he was leaving in a cloud of dust I'd never track down.

I closed my eyes and sighed. Time for the Hail Mary. The cards I was most terrified of playing, the ones that could either make this work or make it even more painful when he turned me away. Forcing myself to meet his eyes again, I said, "You want to know why this scares the shit out of me?"

"Okay...."

I swallowed. "My last two relationships ended badly. And they hurt. Bad enough I swore off anything but casual dating for the foreseeable future." I barely kept myself from wincing at the twin memories.

"And you think I'd do that to you?"

Shaking my head, I said, "It's not that I thought you would do what they did that scared me away. It's the fact that...." I hesitated, then cleared my throat. "It's the fact that I'm more in love with you than I ever was with either of them."

Ryan jumped like I'd slapped him. "You...."

"I'm sorry I hurt you. I'm sorry I walked away. You're the last person in this world I'd want to hurt, and I'm... I'm sorry." I couldn't keep holding his gaze and barely pushed my voice above a whisper as I added, "I love you, Ryan."

His lips parted.

I dropped my gaze. "I was too scared to admit it to myself, and couldn't admit it to you either. I don't want you to stay if you're not happy here with me or with Tucker Springs or both, but if you're going to leave because of me, then... well, I can't stop you. I won't hold you back or tie you down. I just needed you to know why I did what I did, and how I felt. Feel."

He inched a little closer. "You wouldn't be holding me back." He reached up and touched my face, sending a shiver down my spine. "Being with you means I don't have a reason to leave."

My heart melted. I met his gaze, certain he was about to take that back and decide the road was more appealing after all. But as his hand slid from my face into my hair, he leaned closer to me, and I leaned closer to him, and his kiss was... a relief. A breath I'd held too damned long and finally released. I wrapped my arms around him, and he held me against him, every touch of his hand and gentle movement of his lips backing up what he'd said.

The world outside crept back into existence, though, and with it, reality. Plans for the future, directions our lives would or wouldn't go.

I broke the kiss and met his eyes.

"What about Arizona?" I swallowed. "The job… this winter…."

"It's not written in blood." He stroked my cheek. "My uncle will understand if I decide I want to stay."

"And you *do* want to stay?"

A smile slowly formed on his lips as he ran the pad of his thumb back and forth across my cheekbone. "Isn't it obvious?"

I laughed nervously. "Can you break it down for me? Tell me like I'm stupid?"

The smile turned into a grin. Ryan pulled me to him and kissed me.

After a moment he said, "It's kind of funny. I always saw Tucker Springs as just another stop on the road. I'd spend a few months or maybe a year or two here, and then I'd move on." He took my hand in both of his. "But ever since I met you, I've had this feeling that if I ever left this place, sooner or later I'd find my way back."

"I'd be perfectly happy if you never left."

Ryan smiled again. "I'm thinking I could be too."

I reached up and cradled his neck in both hands, and when he leaned down again, I pressed my lips to his. The familiar brush of his goatee against my face settled something inside me, as if I'd needed that last little bit of reassurance that I hadn't just imagined all of this.

The kiss deepened. Ryan's hand slid around the back of my neck, and his grasp tightened as his kiss became more insistent and demanding. Without a crutch or a cast to impede us, we held each other tight, separated only by clothes and body heat.

"I need to take a shower," he said after a while. "Do you want to join me?"

Relief mingled with arousal. "Yes. I definitely do."

CHAPTER SEVENTEEN

WE'D NEVER been closer to each other. Naked, no clothing or plaster or icy distance keeping us apart. Hot water ran over us but not between us, and for the first time I touched him—his face, his chest, his amazing ass—with both hands instead of just one.

His kiss was hungry and demanding this time, the closest it had ever come to forceful, his fingers digging into the back of my neck as he urged my lips apart.

At some point we came up for air, and I whispered, "I missed you."

"I missed you too." Ryan touched his forehead to mine and pulled my body closer to his. "I was angry, but I…. God, I missed you."

"I'm sorry."

"You're here." He kissed me again. "That's all I care about."

He cupped my cheek in one hand, and we just held each other's gazes. Water darkened his hair and slid

down the sides of his face, one droplet running along
the edge of his goatee. Then he drew me in and we
melted into another kiss, bodies pressed together beneath the falling water.

He used his body weight to back me up against
the wall, which held me up as he dipped his head and
kissed my neck. His hard cock pressed against mine.
My knees shook. Both of them. Unhindered and un-
supported by plaster, they threatened to shake right out
from under me as we kissed and ground together.

I nudged him back with a hand on his chest.

"What's—"

"I've been waiting forever to do this," I said, and
carefully went to my knees. I'd been able to suck him
off a few times, but positioning had always been difficult because I couldn't kneel. That, and I'd only had
use of one hand.

Now? Both hands. I could finally use both hands.
I stroked him with both, twisting a little with one while
I teased the head of his cock with my lips and tongue.

He grasped my hair, combed his fingers through it,
grasped it again. "Oh my God," he moaned. "D-don't
make me come. Please."

"I want to."

"I know." He stroked my hair with a shaking hand.
"But I want to fuck you."

"You will." I circled the head of his dick with my
tongue. "We have all night."

"But I... I...." He trailed off into a helpless moan
as I slowly took him into my mouth. "Oh God...." Ryan
whimpered. His hand smacked the tile wall so hard it
startled me, and I almost wasn't ready when the first jet
of semen shot across my tongue. I caught it all, though,
and swallowed without choking.

He kept a hand flat against the wall and rested the other on my shoulders. "Holy... shit...."

I nudged his hand away and rose, and he practically sank against me as I wrapped my arms around his waist and kissed him. Though his body was limp and shaky, his mouth was bold and demanding, and he returned the kiss breathlessly, desperately, the way he always did after I'd given him a blow job.

"Just wait," he slurred between kisses. "Soon as I recover...."

"I can't wait. God, I want you so bad."

Ryan kissed me, but the kiss ended as quickly as it had begun, and he reached past me. The water stopped, and in the sudden silence that followed, his quiet voice seemed to echo off the tiles: "Bedroom."

For the first time there was no cast and no crutch to hinder us, and our hands weren't needed for anything except grabbing on to each other, touching each other, dragging each other toward the bed. Still wet and not giving a single fuck about it, we fell onto the mattress together.

I got on top and pinned his arms beside him, and we kissed so hungrily it bordered on violent. The kissing was out of control. The touches were desperate grasps, both of us practically clawing at each other on top of the sheets.

And he didn't take long to recover. Somewhere in the middle of the panting and groping and making out, he guided my hand between us, and we both gasped as he closed my fingers around his hardening cock.

He stroked me. I stroked him. Our hips moved together, and our mouths moved together, and even our breathing fell into sync.

"Get on your back," he growled, leaning away to get a condom. "So I can fuck you."

Oh God, I loved this aggressive, demanding side of him.

For once all I needed was a single pillow under my hips rather than stacks and mountains to hold my leg in place. Comfortable sex again. Thank God.

Ryan swept his tongue across his lips as he rolled on the condom. Once he had on the condom and no small amount of lube, I spread my legs for him, and he guided himself to me. I was so damned turned on it was painful, so aroused I could barely stand it, and as he pushed against me with his rock-hard cock, I thought I was going to shatter completely because I needed him *so fucking bad.*

Ryan shut his eyes and bit his lip as he pressed into me. My back arched under us. I gripped his arms, desperate for something—anything—to hold on to as he inched deeper inside me. He took a few slow, careful strokes, but once he could move freely without fear of hurting me, he sped up. I spread my legs wider, allowing him deeper, and he felt so fucking good.

Whimpering softly, Ryan leaned down and slid his hands under my back, and he ground against me, and I could *feel* him. All of him. Not only his cock deep inside me, but all of *him.* There was nothing between us, nothing to keep my inner thigh from brushing his hip or both my hands from running through his hair.

I rocked my hips, and Ryan shuddered as his rhythm almost came apart. Then he recovered, and we moved together, and he forced himself so deep I was sure it should have hurt, but oh, God, this was amazing. I moaned again, and he must've thought I was on the verge of crying. I probably was. Hell if I knew. All I knew was how good he felt, how close I was to coming, how much I wanted this to go on and on and on and at the same time didn't think I'd survive another second if I didn't come.

Of course, that was when my leg started to cramp.

I winced and swore under my breath.

"You okay?" he asked, slowing down a little.

I nodded. "Just a… cramp."

Ryan hooked his elbow under my knee, drawing it up enough to relieve the muscle fatigue. "Better?"

"Much."

"Good." He grinned, and then he slammed into me, and he fucked me *hard*. With my leg up that way, the angle was spectacular, and he didn't hold back, didn't do anything except force himself into me again and again until there wasn't a damned thing I could do to keep my climax at bay.

I let go. Completely surrendered. Might have cried out, might have sworn and called his name and sworn again, but all I knew for sure were the intense waves rushing through me and the deep, powerful thrusts that kept my orgasm going and going and going.

Eventually I exhaled hard and relaxed.

He slowed, but he didn't stop. "This okay?"

I nodded. "*Oh*, yeah." Fuck, it was more than okay. I was hypersensitive from my orgasm, and every stroke bordered on way too much, but Ryan was fucking me, so I didn't give a damn about anything else as long as he didn't stop.

He slid his arms under me and buried his face against my neck again. He thrust into me so hard it was painful, and shuddered violently. "Oh… *fuck*."

I held on to him, letting every tremor resonate through my body as well as his, and stroked his hair as he slowly came down.

As soon as his arms were steady, Ryan got up and got rid of the condom. With his back turned, I saw that he still had the familiar Army tattoo.

"You didn't get your new ink?" I asked.

He glanced back and shrugged. "I'm still thinking about it. I like Seth's work, just not ready to commit yet." He smiled. "But later on, I'll show you some of the designs he sent me."

I returned the smile. "Looking forward to it. Maybe if you get yours, I'll finally get mine."

"Oh yeah? You settled on one?"

"That line drawing of the dressage horse has some appeal."

"Fitting." He slid back into bed beside me. "Any idea where you'll get it?"

I shrugged. "Don't know. Not ready to commit to it yet."

Ryan chuckled and wrapped his arms around me. Though the dust seemed to have settled and the easy banter had returned, some of the earlier tension lingered between Ryan's eyebrows, as if there were still something he needed to say.

I brushed a droplet of water from his temple. "What's on your mind?"

He tensed a little and broke eye contact. "There's, um, something that took me a while to figure out. About myself, and about us."

"Oh?"

Ryan moistened his lips. "I told you I move around a lot. Never stay in one place. And when that's all you've ever known, you never really find any one place that's home. You know?"

I nodded. "Yeah, you mentioned that."

"Right." He went on, "I've always envied people who have that. I never thought I could." He paused again, eyes losing focus as if he were collecting his thoughts. "When we met, I was ready to leave Tucker Springs like I've been ready to leave any other place. But that changed after I met you. This place still wasn't anything special, but I... I didn't want to leave anymore." He hesitated, chewing his lip and avoiding my eyes. "And it took me a while to figure out exactly why."

I gulped but didn't speak.

Ryan took a deep breath and finally met my eyes again. He touched my face, drawing a gentle arc across my cheekbone with his thumb. "Tucker Springs isn't home. But I wanted to—want to—stay here because I feel like... anywhere I'm with you could be home."

My heart skipped. "Ryan...."

He touched my face and kissed me tenderly. "I love you, Nathan."

Tears stung my eyes as I pulled him to me for another kiss. "I love you too." I brushed my lips across his. "I'm sorry. For—"

"Don't." He raised his chin and kissed my forehead. "It's done."

"I didn't mean to hurt you, though. I just need you to know that."

Ryan nodded, smiling down at me. "I know. I understand." He leaned down and kissed my cheek. "But you're back now. That's the part that matters."

"Yes, I am." I smoothed his damp hair. "And so are you."

"I am." He grinned. "So, does this mean I can talk you into giving me a few more riding lessons?"

"I don't think you need lessons, to tell you the truth."

"Hmm. Okay, how about just riding?"

Glaring at him playfully, I asked, "Are you using me to get to my horse?"

He batted his eyes. "What can I say? I missed Tsarina." Leaning in to kiss me, he added, "I missed both of you."

"Pretty sure she missed you too. It'll be good for her anyway. I still can't ride yet."

"Still?" Three creases appeared on his forehead. "Isn't your leg healed?"

"It is, but all the muscles atrophied, and nothing wants to bend the way it's supposed to yet." I grinned. "But for the time being, there are worse things to suffer through than watching you riding my horse."

He chuckled. "So we have a deal?"

"Yes, we do." I glanced at the clock beside his bed. "And it's still early. We could go down to the barn."

"Maybe." He ran his fingers through my wet hair. "Or we could go tomorrow."

"We could."

"In the meantime, you want to stay here tonight?"

I trailed the tip of my thumb along the edge of his goatee. "You want me to?"

Ryan smiled. "I'd be perfectly happy if you never left again."

"Careful what you wish for."

He laughed and kissed me gently. "I know exactly what I'm wishing for."

I said nothing. I just pulled him into a lazy, warm embrace and kissed him again.

I had every intention of staying.

Deep down, I hoped he really did too.

CHAPTER EIGHTEEN

I'D NEVER been this nervous around a horse. Never. I was born for the saddle, and I'd had a fearless streak a mile wild ever since my mom leased me that devil pony for 4-H when I was a kid.

Facing Tsarina this time, I was nervous as hell.

The cast had been off for a few weeks now, but the doctor had advised me to stay out of the saddle until I'd regained some strength in my atrophied leg. So I'd visited the physical therapist's chamber of horrors twice a week. I'd also had acupuncture treatments from Mike to stimulate both my hand and my leg.

Now I could walk with a very minimal limp, and though my hand got tired if I wrote or typed for too long, at least I could use it again. For all intents and purposes, I had made a full recovery, and I'd be fine from here on out.

Assuming I didn't do something stupid. Like, say, take another tumble with my horse.

Ryan put a hand on my shoulder. "You don't have to do it today. I can keep riding her until you're ready."

I scowled playfully at him. "You just want her all to yourself."

He laughed and shrugged. "Okay, so I do. But"—the laughter vanished—"really, if you're not ready, don't push yourself."

"No, I can do this." I patted Tsarina's shoulder. "I guess now I know where the expression comes from about getting back on the horse that threw you." I stroked her neck. Her coat was already getting that extra fluffy layer in preparation for a Colorado winter, further proof that the summer she and I were supposed to spend on the trails had come to an end.

"You'll be fine." Ryan kissed my cheek. "As long as no rogue motorcycles wander in here."

I laughed. "Very funny."

He chuckled.

"Okay." I took a deep breath and gathered the reins. I held the stirrup steady and put my foot in it. My leg muscles objected but not too emphatically.

I paused for another breath, for a moment of "okay, I can do this," and then I gritted my teeth and pulled myself up. The muscles protested a bit more vehemently, aching and smarting as my newly healed leg supported most of my weight while I swung the other over Tsarina's back.

In spite of my apprehension and the nightmares I'd had last night about broken bones and limbs in casts, the second I started carefully lowering myself into the saddle, my confidence came back. There were few feelings in the world that compared to sinking into a saddle. The familiar squeak of leather, the perfectly contoured seat, even the way the stirrup leathers pressed into the insides of my knees, it was all exactly the way I remembered it. The braided reins in my hands. The smell of dust and tack and horses. Being back where I belonged, in the saddle that felt less like a place to sit and more like an extension of me. I'd been terrified that being on Tsarina's back would be awkward and strange, but no, it was like the last few months had never happened.

I slipped my right foot into the stirrup and flexed my left ankle a little, stretching my calf and making sure nothing seemed off. Once I was sure I was properly situated, I tapped her sides with my calves, and she started walking.

The first few steps brought a grin right to my lips. Oh yeah. It had sucked missing out on riding her all summer, but this was worth the wait.

I eased her into a sitting trot. Her gait was just like I remembered: glass-smooth. Balanced. Perfect. As I pushed her into a faster trot, I started posting, and the vague ache in my leg was only a minor annoyance. A little bit of muscle fatigue wasn't going to put a damper on the sheer joy of doing this, of the speed and the—

Tsarina suddenly jerked sideways, shying away from the corner. My heart jumped into my throat, but I stayed in the saddle and reined her to a halt.

She snorted loudly at something in the corner. After a moment I heard a faint *cheep-cheep* and some rustling and saw a couple of beaks sticking up from a cluster of twigs.

"Oh, honestly." I tousled her mane. "They're *birds*, sweetheart."

"You all right?" Ryan called from the middle of the arena.

"Yep." I glanced at him and smirked. "Birds again."

He rolled his eyes and shook his head.

Tsarina snorted again but then lost interest in the birds and focused on trying to take a bite out of the railing.

"You dork," I said, chuckling as I steered her away. We made another lap around the arena, and this time passed by the terrifying birds without incident.

I gently tugged the reins with my fingers, enough to wiggle the bit and get her attention, and then urged her into another sitting trot. After a few steps I tapped her side with my leg, and she moved right into that beautiful canter. God, it was like I'd never been out of the saddle at all.

For all my nerves about getting on, by the time we were finished, I didn't want to dismount.

From the sounds coming from the barn, though, it was getting to be feeding time, and Tsarina had definitely noticed. She paid attention and did as she was told but stole a few glances toward the gate too.

I steered her to the middle of the arena and halted beside Ryan. "Guess I should let her go eat."

"Yeah, probably." He grinned up at me. "Looks like you're right at home, aren't you?"

"Yes, I am."

His eyebrows rose a little. "And she's still running the way she should? I didn't ruin her for you?"

"Not even a little." I leaned down and kissed him, which was a challenge because of her height, but he stood up on his toes and met me halfway. "Thank you again. I really appreciate you keeping her in shape for me."

He smiled and kissed me again before letting me sit up in the saddle. Then he stroked the mare's neck. "I guess in a way, you brought us together, didn't you, Tsarina?"

"Good point." I smoothed an unruly piece of her mane. "I suppose we can forgive her for being terrified of a bird's nest, then, right?"

Ryan laughed and stroked her neck. "You know, we could have a bit of a problem."

"What do you mean?"

"There's two of us and one of her. Makes it tough to ride together, don't you think?"

"Okay, true. Maybe Cody has a horse you can ride."

"Maybe." An odd little smile worked the corners of his mouth upward. "But I was thinking I might get one of my own."

I blinked. "Really?"

Ryan nodded, that smile still fixed on his lips.

I didn't push the issue, but it didn't leave my mind. As we unsaddled Tsarina and put her away for the evening, the conversation kept replaying in my head.

Though everything had been amazing since we'd gotten back together, I'd never been able to shake the uneasiness in the back of my mind that it wouldn't last. That while he loved me and everything was perfect now, the fact remained that I was in love with a flight risk, and that terrified me. That we were walking a delicate line, just waiting for something on the horizon to catch his eye.

And with that offhand comment, he'd nudged me off-balance. He'd jarred that delicate line beneath my feet. Maybe it had just been an idle comment. Making conversation and nothing more. Not opening the gate to a deeper discussion about where we were going—or not going—and how willing he was to stay here.

Whatever he meant by it, it kept needling me, so as we walked out of the barn, I cleared my throat. "So, um, do you really want to get a horse of your own?"

Ryan shrugged. "I was thinking about it."

"Seriously?"

He nodded.

We kept walking, but then he glanced at me. "Is, um, something wrong?"

I stopped. So did he. After a moment I faced him. "I guess I'm wondering...." I hesitated, swallowing hard. "You're talking about horses and...." Another moment's hesitation. "But what happens if you get one and then decide you've had enough of Tucker Springs?"

Ryan smiled and cupped my face in one hand. "Then I guess we'll have to get our hands on a two-horse trailer, won't we?" Before I could respond, he kissed me. When he broke the kiss, his expression turned serious. "I want to stay here. I want to be with you."

Part of me wanted to take that at face value and be happy with the answer, but deep down I knew it couldn't be that simple. "But what if you *do* get restless?"

"Then we can travel. Together."

I didn't let myself rest too much hope on that. "Except, I guess, I'm kind of afraid we have the truck keys of Damocles hanging over us."

Ryan nodded. "I understand that. And it's hard to explain why this is different and why you don't need to worry about me running."

"Try me," I said.

His eyes lost focus for a second. Then they met mine. "Listen, I've been out on the road off and on for years, and for the first time I don't feel like there's anything out there that's worth seeing if it means leaving behind what I have here. I don't want to leave you behind." He once again lost focus, but after a moment he went on. "No place has ever been home. I don't know what it's like to feel that way about a place, whether it's a city or a house or whatever." Running his fingers down the side of my cheek, he whispered, "All I know is I feel like I'm home when I'm with you."

Words completely failed me. Hell, breathing failed me. I stared at him, trying to make sense of what he'd said, of what it meant.

"I love you, Nathan," he said. "And I'm not going anywhere."

"I love you too. You know I don't want to tie you down, though. If you want—"

"I don't." He drew me in and, right before our lips met again, whispered, "I'm here with you because I want to be."

As we wrapped our arms around each other, my fear and apprehension melted away. Just like the first moment back in the saddle, I relaxed. I couldn't predict the future, but I wasn't afraid of it anymore.

After all, the future was anyone's guess. If watching Brad and Jeff had taught me anything, it was that nothing—neither the success of a great relationship nor the collapse of a failing one—was certain. And every relationship I'd ever had had felt like it was on a collision course with disaster, that around the next turn was an abrupt drop-off. Like it was going ninety miles an hour toward its own smoking crater.

Now that Ryan had laid it all out and told me how he felt, I didn't feel that way about him. That nagging fear was gone.

Anything could happen. We could go down in flames like millions of well-intentioned couples did. But I was optimistic for the first time. The future was wide open in front of us, a distant horizon at the end of a long strip of highway. Maybe we'd pull this thing off, maybe we wouldn't, but deep down I was sure we could get this right.

If the day came when Ryan needed to ride off into the sunset, then he would.

And I'd be right beside him.

KEEP READING FOR AN EXCERPT FROM

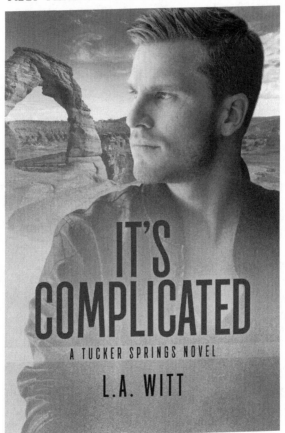

IT'S
COMPLICATED

A TUCKER SPRINGS NOVEL

L.A. WITT

A Tucker Springs Novel

Brad Sweeney and Jeff Hayden have broken up countless times, but now they're starting over from scratch. Finally it seems that they might actually have fixed their problems, taking it a day at a time, dating. Making time for each other. Things look good after a hundredth first date until Jeff's ex-wife and business partner announces she's pregnant—with Jeff's baby.

Brad loves Jeff, and he's determined to make it work. But Jeff's business already puts a lot of demands on his time. Now it looks like Brad will have to compete with a baby too, and contend with the possibility that Jeff is still carrying a torch for his ex.

Then Jeff's ex says she's leaving Tucker Springs— and that leaves Jeff in an untenable situation. He can either do double duty at the shop and share custody between Tucker Springs and Denver, or follow her there. Either way, how can he find room for Brad?

Coming soon to
www.dreamspinnerpress.com

Chapter 1

Brad

I THOUGHT I was nervous on our first date.

Which I had been. God, I'd been a wreck. But tonight? Sitting outside the restaurant, drumming my thumbs on the steering wheel in between texting with my friend Nathan, nervous wreck didn't even begin to describe it. Four years, a few breakups, and over a year of struggling to work things out—complete with multiple false starts—had led up to tonight.

Even if things don't go perfectly, my former roommate, Nathan, sagely said via yet another text, so what? You guys have been trying too long to fix it for one night to screw it up.

He was probably right. If one night could blow this thing out of the water, we'd have been history a long, long time ago. Assuming, of course, this didn't turn out to be the straw that broke the camel's—

Don't think like that, I reminded myself again.

I wrote back to Nathan: OK. He'll be here shortly. I'm heading in.

My thumb hovered over the button, as if the text committed me to getting out and going in, but then I bit the bullet and hit Send. As soon as the message was gone, I stepped out of the car, straightened my jacket, and headed inside.

I hadn't been here before. Neither had Jeff. We'd both agreed it would be fitting to start over in a new place, on unfamiliar ground—a fresh start in every way possible. And besides, it wasn't like we could go to the restaurant where we'd had our first date. Just last year, it had been demolished to make way for a hipster bistro with a vegan menu and poetry slams.

So we'd agreed on the Whitewater Grill. Nathan said his boss had insisted it was good and that the prime rib was utterly spectacular. Guess we'd find out.

The restaurant was dimly lit, almost completely dark except for flickering candles on every small, intimate table. It wasn't coat-and-tie formal, but it was upscale enough I was glad I'd opted for a jacket.

A pretty brunette in a crisp white shirt smiled at me from behind the hostess's podium. "Can I help you, sir?"

"I—yes. I have a seven o'clock reservation for two." When had my mouth gone dry? "Brad Sweeney."

She found the reservation and took me to a table on the far side of the restaurant by the windows, promising to send Jeff over as soon as he arrived. After she'd gone, I opened one of the leather-bound menus, scanning the entrées in between glancing at the front door.

My phone vibrated. This time the message hadn't come from Nathan.

I'm on my way. Will be about 15 min late.

Fifteen minutes? Not bad.

I'm here, I sent back. Should I order wine?

A minute or so later: Get something red. :-) Be there shortly.

I smiled and reached for the wine list. So he really was on his way. Otherwise he'd have told me to wait. He'd be here soon.

Oh God. He would be here soon, wouldn't he?

I took a gulp of ice water. When the waitress came by, I ordered a bottle of cabernet sauvignon. And a refill of water. Another after she'd brought and presented the wine.

I closed my eyes and took a few slow, deep breaths. I was overreacting. It wasn't like this was a first date with a stranger who might be nothing like the description from his online profile or a well-meaning mutual friend. We knew each other. Hell, we already knew each other's irritating quirks and habits. There was no need for first-date bravado and being on our best behavior, even if my fluttering stomach begged to differ.

If anything, this was just a formality. Going out to dinner to mark the first night of trying again. Again. So, no pressure or anything.

Nope, no pressure at all.

Fuck.

The air in the room changed with the opening and closing of the front door. I looked, and my God, he was here.

It was a damned good thing my—our—table was on the opposite side of the room. I needed a moment to get used to him, and it wasn't only because of my nerves. Not this time. We weren't here for a confrontation, and seeing him like this, as my date and not my adversary, took me back to the night we'd met. As he crossed the crowded room, a black blazer hugging his shoulders and a pair of tight jeans hugging his hips, he was every bit the blond-haired, blue-eyed piece of eye candy who'd nearly caused me drop my drink at that party a few years ago. A little bit nervous, a little bit cocky, and a whole lot of oh fuck, please tell me I'm not imagining him.

When he was a few steps away, I stood, not even sure what the protocol was here. A platonic handshake as if we really were strangers? A hug? Fuck, I really sucked at this.

Jeff smiled and, without any hesitation at all, put his hand on my waist and kissed my cheek. "Sorry I'm late."

I laughed in spite of my nerves. "You're always late."

His cheeks colored in the low light. "I really did mean to be here on time, though."

I shrugged and gestured for him to sit. As we took our seats, I said, "Stuck at the shop?"

"Yeah. But we're training Tim up to be our new assistant manager, so hopefully that won't be happening as much anymore."

One can hope, right?

Our eyes met, and we both smiled. Then we picked up our menus and perused them, even though I'd already been through it seventy-eight times and knew exactly what I wanted. At least it was something to do while I got my head around Jeff being on the opposite side of the table.

Jeff settled on something, and we both closed our menus. When the waitress came back, we ordered, and then she was gone... with the menus, which left us with nothing to distract us but a bottle of wine.

Where the hell to start, anyway? We'd hit the ground running on our actual first date, talking from the moment we sat down until the manager kicked us out thirty minutes after closing. Tonight? Crickets.

"So." Jeff cleared his throat. "I, uh, guess we don't have to go through the motions of hobbies, favorite movies, and all of that."

I laughed. "No, I think we've got that pretty well covered."

"Yeah, we do." His eyebrows flicked upward. The unspoken question didn't help the nervousness in my gut: So what do we talk about?

As the flickering candlelight played on his features, we locked eyes. It was weird to see him like this. For the last few months, every dinner we'd shared had been in the name of keeping this thing alive, and the tension had been reminiscent of a treaty negotiation. Tonight, though, we were here on different terms. But where the hell did we start?

"So how are things at the shop?" I wasn't crazy about discussing work over dinner, especially that fucking shop, but it was something.

Jeff ran a finger along the edge of the placemat. "Busy. And it's been a little crazy since I started adjusting my hours."

"Oh yeah? How is that going?"

He shrugged. "It's going. I'm training one of the guys to handle—" He dropped his gaze, laughing a little as his cheeks flushed. "I already said that, didn't I?" Before I could respond, he cleared his throat. "Anyway, Tim's picking up more responsibilities, and I've even been eating lunch at my desk so I can still get things done."

"Jeff." I eyed him. "Cutting your hours doesn't mean cutting out all your breaks."

He shook his head. "No, it's not that bad. I just catch up on emails and invoices. Stuff like that."

"As long as you're not killing yourself."

"I'm not." He smiled. "I promise. I'm scaling things back. Though cutting my hours has been weird. Not bad, but weird."

"So Christine didn't mind it?"

Jeff shook his head. "No, she understood. In fact, she's doing the same thing. I mean, I could never in a million years convince her to work less than a sixty-hour week, but she's got an ironclad day off every week now."

"That's good to hear. She needs it."

"She does. And once Tim is ready, she and I can scale back more." His forehead creased. "It'll take some time, but I'm trying. I promise."

"I know." I smiled. "You can't completely rearrange your life overnight."

Jeff's long workdays had been one of many bones of contention, and God bless the man, he'd been making a hell of an effort to spend less time at work. A huge time commitment came with the territory of owning a business, which I absolutely understood, but even he agreed we stood a better chance at making this work if he wasn't coming home at midnight and leaving again at six.

He reached for his wineglass. "So what's going on with— What the hell?" He shoved a hand into his pocket, and as soon as he'd pulled out his phone, I recognized Christine's distinctive ringtone. Glaring at the screen, he muttered, "Goddamn it, Chris. Seriously?"

I picked up my own glass and slowly swirled my wine. "If you need to take it, go ahead."

Jeff shook his head and declined the call. "No. I want my job to interfere less with us. That starts tonight." He fiddled with the phone again, probably putting it on silent, and put it back in his pocket.

"But what if Christine—"

"No." Jeff put up a hand. "She knows. She understands."

"Except she just tried to call you."

"Whatever it is, she'll handle it." He cracked one of those sly grins that had always made me weak. "And if nothing else, she'll yell at me when I go in on Sunday."

I laughed. "I have no doubt about that." We both knew she wouldn't really yell at him—no other ex-spouses on the planet, business partners or not, could calmly hash things out like Jeff and Christine—but she'd certainly let him know if she was unhappy.

"Anyway." Jeff's hand made it all the way to his wineglass this time. "As I was about to ask before we were rudely interrupted, how are things at work?"

"Oh, you know. The usual retail shit. Though the other day…."

JUST LIKE on our first date, we kept talking until long after the food was gone. Wrapped up in each other, enjoying this easy, relaxed conversation after months on end of fighting and cold silences, neither of us seemed to be in any hurry to stop.

I didn't want the night to be over. In part because it was so good to be like this with Jeff again, but admittedly, there was a little more to it than that. We were in a weird place between dating and not, between something completely new and something we'd long ago broken in, and neither of us really knew the rules. We'd eventually figured out how to start the evening, but how in the world did we end it?

First dates were usually something to play by ear. A kiss? A handshake? A blow job in the back seat? Waking up together the morning after? That was half the fun of a first date—anything was possible.

Jeff and I, though, we had to handle things a little more delicately. Aside from a brief platonic embrace each time we'd said goodbye, and that kiss on the cheek earlier, we hadn't touched in months. Sex blurred lines and complicated everything. I didn't want to fall into bed with him and risk the temptation of sticking around just because the sex was good, so we'd kept each other physically at arm's length while we tried to get closer emotionally. We had both stayed in miserable relationships because we enjoyed the sex, and we'd both regretted it. Not this time. No sex until we'd worked the kinks out of everything else.

But holding each other's gazes across the table, chuckling over the rims of our wineglasses as we leaned over the places our plates had been a couple of hours before, I was tempted. Holy fuck, I was tempted. I'd forgotten how his blue eyes could make my head spin faster than the wine in my glass could.

And when he reached across the table and put his hand over mine, the effect was like a magnet to a hard drive. My mind went completely blank. Whatever we'd been talking about just then—gone.

Jeff looked down at our hands and quickly withdrew his. "Sorry," he muttered and went for his wineglass.

Don't be.

"It's okay." I smiled and hoped to God he couldn't hear my pounding heart and that he hadn't suddenly developed X-ray vision that would let him see through the table to the effect that simple touch had had on me. "Old habits die hard, right?"

"Yeah." He laughed, though it sounded forced. "Guess they do." He broke eye contact, cleared his throat, and glanced at something behind me. "I think we'd better go." He chuckled. "Our waitress has checked her watch about six times in the last five minutes. I think the poor girl wants to go home."

"Oh. Is it that late already?" According to my cell phone, it was almost eleven. "Wow. Yeah, I guess we should go."

Jeff flagged down the waitress and asked for the check, and while we waited, he faced me again and smiled. "I guess this is the part where I tell you I had a good time and nervously ask if we can do this again?"

I smirked. "Does that mean it's the part where I act all coy and tell you to call me later this week so you have to figure out where the line is between too soon and too late?"

Jeff laughed, which didn't do much to unscramble my thoughts. "To be serious, I think tonight was a good start. We really should, um, do this again."

"We should." Relief rushed through me, even though his comment brought to life a whole new set of nerves. Yeah, we'd pulled this off once, passed with flying colors and not fucked things all up again, but could we swing it a second time? Only one way to find out. "My evenings are free when I'm not working a closing shift. Tell me when and where."

"We'll make it happen."

We split the check and each left a generous tip to make up for occupying the table for so long. The manager locked the door behind us after we'd stepped outside, and Jeff and I walked in silence down the wooden stairs to the mostly deserted gravel lot.

We were halfway to our cars—his truck was parked two spaces over from my Camry—when he stopped.

I stopped too and faced him, thinking he might've forgotten his keys or his phone inside. Wouldn't be the first time, and a little playful nostalgia brought a smile to my lips as I remembered that running joke. *What'd you forget this time?* I almost asked.

But then I realized he wasn't searching his pockets, and he wasn't looking anywhere except right at me. As he drew in a deep breath, one of those slow and deliberate ones that meant he was about to say something important, my stomach somersaulted.

"Listen, I…." His eyes flicked toward the ground between us, then met mine again. "I meant what I said in there. I really do want to see you again."

I swallowed. "Me too."

Gravel crunched beneath his feet as he shifted his weight. "There's another new place down by one of the universities. Indian restaurant. I, um, I've heard it's pretty good. Maybe we could give it a try?"

"I think I've heard about the one. Let's go."

"When's good for you?"

The sooner the better. I tried not to fidget, but it was a struggle. "How does your weekend look?"

"I need to work on Sunday, but otherwise…."

"This is my weekend off. Maybe we could try that place tomorrow night?"

"Good idea." He smiled. Then faltered a little. "So, for tonight, do we…." He broke eye contact and cleared his throat.

"Hmm?"

Jeff pushed his shoulders back and met my eyes again. "Since we're starting over and this is technically our first date, does that mean we get another first kiss too?"

All the air left my lungs. "I, uh, guess we get to make our own rules. If we want one, then…."

He held my gaze. Then he narrowed the space between us by half a step, ratcheting my pulse upward. "Then maybe I'm asking the wrong question."

I gulped. "So what should you be asking?"

His hand entered my peripheral vision, nearing my face slowly, cautiously, and I couldn't look anywhere but right at Jeff until his fingertips brushed my cheek and I closed my eyes.

"I guess I should ask…." His thumb drew a gentle arc across my cheekbone. "I should…."

I opened my eyes and met his. *Just ask. I promise I'll say yes.*

He didn't ask.

He drew me in, pressed his lips to mine, and turned my world on its ass.

L.A. WITT and her husband have been exiled from Spain and sent to live in Maine because rhymes are fun. She now divides her time between writing, assuring people she is aware that Maine is cold, wondering where to put her next tattoo, and trying to reason with a surly Maine coon. Rumor has it her archnemesis, Lauren Gallagher, is also somewhere in the wilds of New England, which is why L.A. is also spending a portion of her time training a team of spec ops lobsters. Authors Ann Gallagher and Lori A. Witt have been asked to assist in lobster training, but they "have books to write" and "need to focus on our careers" and "don't you think this rivalry has gotten a little out of hand?" They're probably just helping Lauren raise her army of squirrels trained to ride moose into battle.

Website: www.gallagherwitt.com
Email: gallagherwitt@gmail.com

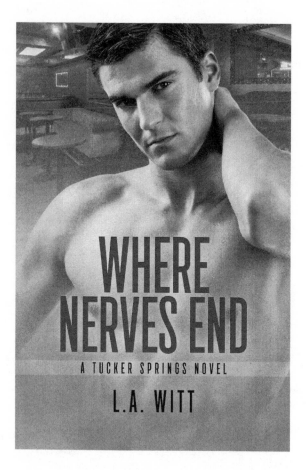

WHERE
NERVES END

A TUCKER SPRINGS NOVEL

L.A. WITT

A Tucker Springs Novel

Welcome to Tucker Springs, Colorado, where you'll enjoy beautiful mountain views and the opportunity to study at one of two prestigious universities—if you can afford to live there.

Jason Davis is in pain. Still smarting from a bad breakup, he struggles to pay both halves of an overwhelming mortgage and balance the books at his floundering business. As if the emotional and financial pain weren't enough, the agony of a years-old shoulder injury keeps him up at night. When he faces a choice between medication and insomnia, he takes a friend's advice and gives acupuncture a try.

Acupuncturist Michael Whitman is a single dad striving to make ends meet, and his landlord just hiked the rent. When new patient Jason, a referral from a mutual friend, suggests a roommate arrangement could benefit them both, Michael seizes the opportunity.

Getting a roommate might be the best idea Jason's ever had—if it weren't for his attraction to Michael, who seems to be allergic to wearing shirts in the house. Still, a little unresolved sexual tension is a small price to pay for pain and financial relief. He'll keep his hands and feelings to himself since Michael is straight… isn't he?

www. dreamspinnerpress.com

SECOND
HAND

A TUCKER SPRINGS NOVEL
MARIE SEXTON
HEIDI CULLINAN

A Tucker Springs Novel

Paul Hannon flunked out of vet school. His fiancée left him. He can barely afford his rent, and he hates his house. About the only things he has left are a pantry full of his ex's kitchen gadgets and a lot of emotional baggage. He could really use a win—and that's when he meets El.

Pawnbroker El Rozal is a cynic. His own family's dysfunction has taught him that love and relationships lead to misery. Despite that belief, he keeps making up excuses to see Paul again. Paul, who doesn't seem to realize that he's talented and kind and worthy. Paul, who's not over his ex-fiancée and is probably straight anyway. Paul, who's so blind to El's growing attraction, even asking him out on dates doesn't seem to tip him off.

El may not do relationships, but something has to give. If he wants to keep Paul, he'll have to convince him he's worthy of love—and he'll have to admit that attachment might not be so bad after all.

www. dreamspinnerpress.com

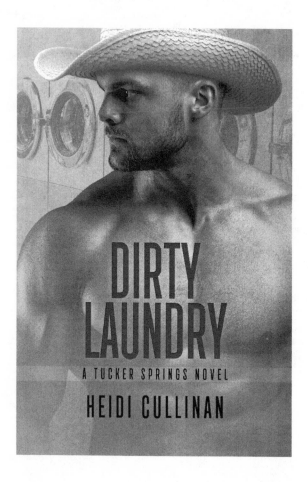

DIRTY LAUNDRY

A TUCKER SPRINGS NOVEL

HEIDI CULLINAN

A Tucker Springs Novel

Sometimes you have to get dirty to come clean.

When muscle-bound Denver Rogers effortlessly dispatches the frat boys harassing grad student Adam Ellery at the Tucker Springs laundromat, Adam's thank-you turns into impromptu sex over the laundry table. The problem comes when they exchange numbers. What if Adam wants to meet again and discovers Denver is a high-school dropout with a learning disability who works as a bouncer at a local gay bar? Or what if Denver calls Adam only to learn while he might be brilliant in the lab, outside of it he has crippling social anxiety and obsessive-compulsive disorder?

Either way, neither of them can shake the memory of their laundromat encounter. Despite their fears of what the other might think, they can only remember how good the other one feels. The more they get together, the kinkier things become. They're both a little bent, but in just the right ways.

Maybe the secret to staying together isn't to keep things clean and proper. Maybe it's best to keep their laundry just a little bit dirty.

www. dreamspinnerpress.com

COVET THY
NEIGHBOR

A TUCKER SPRINGS NOVEL

L.A. WITT

A Tucker Springs Novel

Welcome to Tucker Springs, Colorado, where sparks fly when opposites attract—but are some obstacles too great to overcome?

When tattoo artist Seth Wheeler meets his new neighbor, it's like a revelation. Darren Romero is everything Seth wants in a man: hot, clever, single, and interested. For a minute he seems perfect. Then Darren drops the bomb: he moved to Tucker Springs to be a pastor at the New Light Church.

As a gay man whose parents threw him out, Seth has a strict policy of keeping believers at arm's length for self-preservation. But Darren's perseverance and the chemistry bubbling between them steadily wear down his defenses.

In a small town like Tucker Springs, Seth can't avoid Darren—or how much he wants him. Which means he needs to decide what's more important: protecting himself, or his feelings for his neighbor.

www. dreamspinnerpress.com

NEVER
A HERO

A TUCKER SPRINGS NOVEL

MARIE SEXTON

A Tucker Springs Novel

Owen Meade is in need of a hero. Sheltered, ashamed, and ridiculed by his own mother for his sexuality, his stutter, and his congenital arm amputation, Owen lives like a hermit, rarely leaving his apartment. He hardly dares to hope for more… until veterinarian Nick Reynolds moves in downstairs.

Charming, handsome Nick steals past Owen's defenses and makes him feel almost normal. Meeting his fiery, determined little sister, June, who was born with a similar amputation, helps too. June always seems to get her way—she even convinces Owen to sign up for piano lessons with her. Suddenly the only thing standing between Owen and his perfect life is Nick. No matter how much he flirts, how attracted to Owen he seems to be, or how much time they spend together, Nick always pulls away.

Caught between his mother's contempt and Nick's stubbornness, Owen makes a decision. It's time to be the hero of his own story, and that means going after what he wants: not just Nick, but the full life he deserves.

www. dreamspinnerpress.com